PRAISE FOR

"*Only Son* collapses generations, fuses ti
delicate, fervent book about fatherhood
power of a spiritual text, one quietly ⌐⌐⌐⌐⌐
wonder, promise, and loss."

—Heidi Julavits, author of *Directions to Myself*

"To those who have ever been the bewildered child of a parent or the bewildered parent of a child, I'd like to recommend this remarkable book by Kevin Moffett. With great humor and tenderness, and without platitude or sentimentality, Moffett ingeniously melds the coming-of-age novel, the fatherhood novel, and the road novel. I dislike the thought of anyone calling this book slim or slender—there's just so much life in it, so much mystery."

—Chris Bachelder, author of *The Throwback Special*

"Kevin Moffett's *Only Son* perfectly captures the long ache of fatherhood in all its baffling beauty. It's an extraordinary book about the sometimes tender, sometimes distant, always mysterious relationship between fathers and sons, written with wit and warmth and just enough sting to make it real."

—Nathan Hill, author of *The Nix*

"*Only Son* is a great, glorious siren song of desperation and double helixes—at once a love story and an elegy, a ballad of skate parks and snake nests, the swamp and the desert, bullies and borderlands. It's a chronicle of imperfect attempts to the people standing right in front of us, living in our bones and marrow—and offering them the grace of seeing them differently. This book gripped me and didn't let me go. I read it standing at a rental-car counter and looked up to find half an hour had passed, realized that I would walk away from that Alamo counter in Cincinnati a different woman than the one who'd arrived—reconfigured and oddly resurrected by this tale of sweat, surrender, longing, fathers, sons, ghosts, voicemails, highways, silences, laughter, and—above all—the surprises of life."

—Leslie Jamison, author of *The Empathy Exams*

ONLY SON

McSWEENEY'S
SAN FRANCISCO

Copyright © 2025 Kevin Moffett

All rights reserved, including right of reproduction in whole or in part, in any form.

McSweeney's and colophon are registered trademarks of McSweeney's, a nonprofit publisher based in San Francisco.

ISBN: 978-1-963270-30-3

Cover by Sunra Thompson

10 9 8 7 6 5 4 3 2 1

www.mcsweeneys.net

Printed in the United States

ONLY SON

KEVIN MOFFETT

McSWEENEY'S
SAN FRANCISCO

For my father, in memoriam, and my mother, in Florida.

1.

AN EDUCATION

I can never get the straight story. I mean, I can never get the story straight. They come for his belongings either before his funeral or right after it. I'm either absent or present. His mother and sister—my grandmother and aunt—pack everything: shirts, pants, ties, shoes, childhood pictures, high school yearbooks, golf clubs, tools, even the tan faux-leather recliner he always napped in. They ship it from our house in Florida to their house in Kentucky. Or they rent a moving truck and drive it there. They either think they're being helpful or know they're being selfish. He was theirs before he was ours, they think. The recliner was a birthday gift from my grandmother, so technically it's hers. The shirts and pants and ties are already out of style. They're just forlorn reminders—we're better off with them someplace else. No nine-year-old boy needs eight pairs of Sansabelt slacks and size-eleven FootJoy golf cleats. A clean slate, that's what we need. My mother never objects. Or she silently objects. She's secretly happy they hauled it away. She's too bereft to be secretly anything.

They neglect to take two things: a powder-blue cardigan and an old adding machine. These are my father's remains. The sweater hangs in a hall closet, awaiting orders. The adding machine occupies a shelf next to the television in the living room, a remnant from a vanished civilization. I look at it. I wonder if he ever added anything up with it. He worked as the manager of a horse racing track. *He fell in love with horses and numbers in college...* this is a sentence I will hear again and again from the people who knew my father, until they die. Do you remember much about him? they'll ask, and when I mumble and hedge, they will tell me things.

He was a stellar golfer with the most natural swing. He made it look effortless, a friend of his from the track tells me. His name's Zell. We're at the third hole of a golf course, waiting to tee off. I've never played—by the time I was old enough, my father was too sick to take me—and I am terrible. I whiff so many tee shots that I finally club the ground and shout *motherfuck*. Zell looks like he's sizing me up to fight me. He ends our round on the tenth hole.

Are those your only pair of shoes? he asks me on our way home.

Before he leaves he writes my mom a check for fifty dollars with *sneakers* written in the memo line.

I remember little from before he died and nearly everything afterward. It's as if we switch places: I enter the world just as he departs. I'm stunned, I'm always frustrated and anxious, but I'm not overly sad. Death for now is flowers on the kitchen table and people being slightly nicer to me. My mother letting me do as I please. I stay home from school for days and watch television, resting my foot on the side and changing channels with my toe. I like whatever's on: Falcon Crest, baseball games. Friends and family come and go. My teacher stops by and gives my mother a manila envelope full of cards from my classmates. My name's misspelled on some, words are missing. *Everyone's real sorry what happened.* I read the cards in bed, pore over them the way I used to pore over the backs of baseball cards. A weird sallow girl named Darlene has drawn a blackbird flying above the words *My dads dead too.*

Did you like my card? she asks me later at school. I tell her I did. I say it made me feel better.

She hesitates, as if that wasn't necessarily her intention, then finally says, That's nice. She always has a piece of green gum in her mouth. You can see it whenever she speaks.

Later Darlene tells me her dad didn't really die. He just ran off to Ohio with some woman he met on an airplane.

* * *

My mother is thirty-nine years old. She has one dependent, a neurotic poodle, seven hundred dollars in savings, monthly social security checks. She drinks from bulbous jugs of cheap Gallo wine, smokes Benson & Hedges 100s, and eats one meal a day. She continues wearing her engagement ring until her friend Bunny encourages her to take it off. They say the grieving process lasts six months for every year you were together, Bunny says. My mother has other keepsakes: some pictures, a few postcards he sent from a trip to California, a yellowed slip of paper with his name written in neat cursive. After their first date she wrote it down and wedged it between her mattress and box spring because she heard that's what Janet Leigh did the night she met Tony Curtis.

A month after the funeral she starts looking for a new job. She could return to the horse track, where she worked at a betting window, but she doesn't want to. She finds a job at a cemetery selling burial plots over the phone. Does she find this even remotely comical? She does not. She reads from a script. Usually the person on the other end of the line hangs up before she can read the first sentence: *Look, Mr./Ms./Mrs. _____, I'm well aware that no one likes thinking about themselves or their loved ones dying...* She quits and takes a job selling water softeners and then a job as a teller at a drive-thru bank window. Finally she returns to the horse track, where everyone seems so plodding and glib, brimming with false light. She starts taking night classes at the community college.

The counselor asks if I ever feel angry for no reason. I pause like I'm considering the question and say, Not really.

It isn't a test, he says. It's just two friends talking.

He reads words from a list and asks me to draw pictures, whatever comes to mind, so I draw the things furthest from my mind. If he says *rest* and I think of rain, I draw an octopus. If he says *time* and I think of Time magazine, I draw a man's face. When I'm finished the counselor and I stare at it: vacant eyes, neutral mouth, stump of neck. It looks like a police-sketch assailant, a man sewn together from pieces of other men. There's nothing remotely alive in the face at all.

I know it's a test. I know I'm doing poorly.

How about *love?* the counselor asks.

I remember nothing of the funeral except my mother's breath. It took place in a church, I assume. People came. Conciliatory things were said. I remember being presented with a folded-up flag like a veteran's widow. If I strain I can feel the heft of it in my lap... but that can't be right. At some point, either before the service began or when it was about to end, my mother leaned to me and whispered, *It'll be starting soon.* Or, *It'll be over soon.*

Her breath, I can separate it into tracks: curdled stomach-warm air and cigarette tar and a vague brine of sadness. Alive, fiercely alive, and dead. It startled me awake. An involuntary memory, sealed in wax like a song.

In Kentucky my grandmother and aunt hold a second funeral at their Baptist church. We are not invited. They unpack his belongings and store them in the house he grew up in. Shirts and ties in the closet of his old bedroom, sweaters in the dresser drawer, high school graduation photo on the nightstand. He is theirs again. For my birthday they mail me a framed square of quilting with my name and a Bible verse on it: *For God so loved the world...* They include a check to help pay for a bus ticket to visit them.

They also take his physical remains. Pack him into an airtight container and ship him to Kentucky in the luggage compartment of an airplane. This, too, is never discussed. I don't even think to ask where he's buried until months later when our class visits a cemetery to do headstone rubbings. His final resting place is a family plot in Shelbyville alongside my grandmother's people, distant relatives with names like Mintie and Attaway. My grandfather is buried in some other plot with his people. Here's what I know about my grandfather: he came from hog people. That's all my grandmother has told me. His people were hog people, she said. My people were cow people. To her it explains everything that needs to be explained about him. She is not so forthcoming about my father. Even before he died, she was stingy with her remembrances. Every so often she'd skim some froth for me and keep the good stuff for herself. Now she is silent. When his name is brought up, she closes her eyes as if praying.

The spaces his belongings occupied fill with other belongings. The marks his faux-leather recliner left in the carpet are vacuumed into oblivion. Everything seems to contract around his absence. Our poodle, Linda, hides under my parents' bed for weeks. We slide food and water bowls to her. She growls when we try to lure her out. I sit in my room paging through World War II encyclopedias, looking at photos of charred cityscapes. One shows a man and two girls in Hiroshima, stunned, clothes shredded, surrounded by smoke and rubble. The caption says they lived five miles from ground zero. I return to the photo again and again. It evokes a feeling of sorrow so intense and complete it's almost pleasurable.

My mother goes to bed before I do. Her room is above the living room, and one night I hear her thumping on the floor. The television must be too loud. I turn it down but the thumping continues. Another night as I'm falling asleep I hear someone say my name in the hallway, loud and clear, unmistakable. I get up and check, and Linda's there sniffing at the carpet. It's always at night. Whispering outside the window, rustling in the kitchen, loitering behind closed doors. My father keeps watch and keeps watching until we fade. I sleep with a light on.

Sometimes I can summon his voice: a thin, distant rasp. *One hand grenade could kill us all...* he'd say when people were standing too close. *Go look for me in the other room...* when I was annoying him. Childhood is a song you hear so many times you stop listening to the words. *Let us cross the river and rest under the shade of the trees.* Probably half the things my father said to me he never said to me.

We move to a new town house. The sign at the entrance: LAKE-BRIDGE ESTATES: PEACEFUL COASTAL LIVING. To remind us. A dozen tracts of identical gravy-brown town houses next to a man-made lake. Our unit has a view of a distant windowless building with twenty chimneys, where I'm pretty sure they're incinerating pets. All the missing dogs and cats in town, this is where they end up. I know it. The air at night always smells kind of scorched and furry. The town house is cheaply built. You can't sneeze without someone knowing. You can't cry on the toilet without someone knowing. I sleep in a baby's room beneath a big smiling whale painted on the wall. He looks deranged, like he would destroy your boat just to have someone to play with for a little while. The carpet reeks of stale menthol cigarettes. In the man-made lake are two alligators, Smokey and Kermit. Beneath our back porch is a den of cottonmouths. In the trees are livid owls. The circle of life, below us, above us, hidden in the pores of our bones, invisible.

A friend gives her a copy of When Bad Things Happen to Good People. It sits on a bookshelf in my new room. I scan its title probably a thousand times. It helps me fall asleep if I imagine it as a jingle: *Bad things happen to good people in monsoons, hot-air balloons. Ancient tombs, hospital rooms.* Did the bad thing happen to my father, I wonder, or is it happening to us? And what makes us particularly good? Not once am I tempted to take the book off the shelf and find out.

The wildfires come late that summer. Miles north of us, the pinewoods burn for weeks, clotting the coast of Florida with resinous smoke. We're told to remain indoors. We do as we're told. Outside the windows, pine ash falls and falls, and I play with Star Wars action figures. I'm not allowed to see the movies. I scare too easily. I invent my own story about heroic Darth Vader and his war against the stars. His helmet gives him a sad look: triangle mouth, dead black eyes. I imagine the war is going poorly. A friend tells me that he's the villain and the stormtroopers are his henchmen. I reject it. My Star Wars has no bad guys. The action figures fight side by side against the stars, always overhead but too distant to attack. They curse them from my bedroom carpet.

Finally it rains and I'm allowed to go outside again with the other hostile fauna. Friends and I hunt snakes in the palmetto scrub around our town house. I come home one night covered in chigger bites, and my mother brushes clear nail polish over the welts. I lie shirtless and miserable as the chiggers suffocate in their hidey-holes. My body is a decoy, a trap made of meat. I scratch off the scabs of dried polish one by one. I watch the retired bail bondsman next door decapitate a cottonmouth with a shovel. The snake's severed head keeps snapping while its headless body slithers away, and the retired bail bondsman grins and gestures with the shovel as if he's orchestrated this educational display just for me.

I watch television until it feels like a punishment. I watch soap operas, religious cartoons, after-school specials. All my favorite movies depict growing up as a blossoming, a slow unveiling of what's already there. Maybe it is for some. For me it is work, the daily chore of fashioning myself into something I can live with. So little to excavate, so much to bury. I watch The Terry Fox Story whenever it comes on, scene after scene of that beleaguered

Canadian running through the provinces on a prosthetic leg. Running a marathon a day after his cancer diagnosis to raise money for research. I know I could do something remarkable if I went blind or found out I was dying or had to have one of my limbs amputated, but maybe under no other circumstances.

An older neighbor kid steals my BMX bike and spray-paints it gold. Slowly he pedals around the cul-de-sac, an Olympian flaunting his medal, gloating. I wave to him. What else can I do? My mother sends me up to the 7-Eleven with a note saying it's okay to buy her a carton of cigarettes, and I see Wes Abbot in the parking lot. Wes's dad is locked up at Raiford for involuntary manslaughter. I'm not clear on the definition of involuntary manslaughter, but I'm pretty sure it means he slaughtered another man without meaning to, so I'm wary, even terrified, of Wes. He wears citrus-colored dress shirts and has that forlorn attachment to dogs you see in kids whose parents won't let them have one. He knows all the breeds, remembers the name of every single dog he meets. Wes calls out to me, Sorry about your dad. A strange quality in his voice that will take me years to recognize as sincerity. A simple kindness I will not forget. In the moment, though, all I feel is embarrassment, the indignity of being seen. You too, I say to him.

In the back pages of Mad magazine is an advertisement for the Olympic Sales Club. *Captain O needs kids like you to join his sales army and earn famous name prizes!* There are dozens of illustrated prizes—electric organ, two-man boat, portable TV—and the number of items you must sell to win them. I've seen it before, but this time I notice the stereo system. Belt-drive turntable, Pioneer receiver, hi-fi speakers. The price: 190 items. I stare at the picture, imagining it on my bookshelf with a sheaf of records beneath it, with the one that's currently playing pulled out a little from the rest like my friend Manav does with his. I've wanted a stereo for years. I asked for one for my birthday, and my mother bought me a portable tape recorder, the sort of thing you find in an elementary school library. I listen to music on my clock radio, waiting with the tape recorder for songs I like. At night I bring the clock radio and tape recorder under my covers, waiting for The Devil Went Down to Georgia to come on. After nine p.m., stations play the version where Johnny calls the devil a son of a bitch instead of a son of a gun, and the jolt it gives me is as close as I've come to religion.

I call the Olympic Sales Club's toll-free number and ask for Sally, like the ad tells me. This is Sally, the woman says. What's your name? In the bottom corner of the ad there's an illustration of Sally wearing a generic superhero suit and telephone headset, and I stare at her as we're talking.

She's sending me a sales catalog today. She writes down my address and zip code. She tells me Florida's an untapped market, so I should have an easy time selling items. I don't ask what the items are, or how I might go about selling them. I'm dreaming of hi-fi music, mesmerized to be having a conversation with someone from the back pages of Mad magazine. Captain O can't do this without kids like you, she says. I am not clear on what *this* is, but I'm grateful to be joining an army of kids like me.

I wait for my sales catalog to arrive. I become a connoisseur of boredom. I quit baseball, then balanced meals, dental hygiene, raising my hand, crying, clapping, and all the obsessive counting rituals I used to do to keep him from dying. I go to school. I write sentences as punishment. I wear lightning-bolt socks and draw circle-As on my folders like everyone else. Some kid asks if I know what it stands for, and I say, Sure, I mean, of course I do. But I can't really explain it.

Bahhh, he says. Like a sheep.

Turns out the circle-A stands for anarchy. Who knows why there are so many anarchists at a beach-town elementary school in Florida, but soon it's replaced by a different symbol, and kids quit wearing lightning-bolt socks, and I quit too.

Then there is Yancy, who wears a porkpie hat and khaki fishing vest to school with a homemade tag above the breast pocket that says, SOCIOPATHIC BASS KILLER, and another that says, LEGALIZE CANNIBALISM. He lives within a mile of me, goes to the same school, breathes the same scummy coastal air, and yet has somehow emerged fearless, not just his clothes but his ability to weave eccentricities into camouflage, walking from class to class singing while the rest of us mope bewildered into the middle distance, feeling vaguely like we're being fattened up for something terrible—*singing*, aloud but to himself. And later when I read about Stalin protecting Pasternak, saying, *Don't touch this cloud-dweller*, I'll think of Yancy—even his name sounds celestial, a visitor. He keeps a single porcelain teacup in his backpack. In math class, while the teacher solves practice problems on the board, Yancy catches my eye, nods, reaches into backpack, lifts the teacup in a toast, and waits for me to return it.

New Year's morning, wandering in the deep woods behind our house, I find a switchblade knife in a crumpled lunch bag. It's probably the best day of my life up to this point. I also find, rolled up and stashed in a pine hollow, a porno magazine full of pregnant women. I leaf through it feeling terrible. Instantly, permanently stained. Later I call a phone-sex hotline from the back pages and make my voice deep. Someone picks up and I say hello. I ask her how she's doing. She clears her throat for a long time and says, Well, well, well, Mr. Motherfucker. I've been waiting to hear from you...

Watching an old man pushing a stroller with an oxygen tank where a baby should be. Trying to decipher the sign next to Café Risqué: WE DARE. WE BARE. ALL. Standing on a shell midden during a field trip, and the guide saying, The Timucua lived here a thousand years before Florida was Florida. Imagining a Florida that wasn't Florida. Realizing how inseparable things are to what we call them. My grandmother on my mother's side moved here as a child from New York City in the 1920s. Her father died of galloping consumption soon after that. Ever since then she's imagined death as a horse that sleeps hidden in the day and feeds all night.

On the school bus a kid writes BLACK SABBATH RULES on the back of the seat, and every day I return to see if they've written anything else. I want a list. I want to know exactly what the Black Sabbath rules are.

An awful thing is when they kill the alligator. Five neighborhood boys use meat to lure it out of the man-made lake and tie rope around its snout and then bludgeon it to death with aluminum baseball bats. I watch from a distance. I can't tell whether it's Kermit or Smokey. I see the kid who stole my bike holding the alligator's tail. Lure, tie, bludgeon: it sounds quick and orderly, but the alligator dies slowly. Miserably. Fewer than five kids and it might have escaped or dismembered one of them. When they finish they push its corpse into the lake with its snout still bound shut. The whole scene fills me with disgust and anger, but I can't help but marvel at how coordinated they were. They must've been planning it for days. Studying the alligator's habits, buying meat, gathering baseball bats. The scene plays again and again as I'm trying to fall asleep. It becomes indelible. And I still can't come up with anything I want even half as much as those kids wanted to kill that alligator.

Over spring break a girl dies off-roading on her four-wheeler. There's a moment of silence in class. I bow my head and try to think about her. She once stared me down in the hall and said, Can't touch this, for no reason I could ascertain. My thoughts drift to my father, me coming home to find him napping on the couch a few weeks before he died. He did not look calm. He looked distressed. Rigid. It was the first and last time I ever saw him asleep. Then a kid in the back of the classroom starts making engine revving noises, and others join in, and the moment of silence is over.

Animals, our teacher calls us. Tears in his eyes.

FLORIDA: THE RULES ARE DIFFERENT HERE, the billboards say. To remind us.

What am I waiting for? What higher order? Everybody is trying to teach me a lesson but I am, it would seem, a slow learner. I have finally awoken, I remember every day like it's my last, but I'm still perfecting my holding pattern.

I dream I've killed someone and can't remember where I left the body. Panicked, pacing the woods with a shovel as the sun rises. I tell the counselor I don't remember my dreams. I say I always look forward to going to school. He asks me to write my friends' names on the chalkboard in his office, and since I have only two—Manav and Army, names that look fake as I write them down—I invent some more. He points to one: Tell me about him.

His dad owns a car wash, I say. He points to another and asks what his father does. Repairs things, I say. He's a repairer.

Everyone gets a plausible father. The counselor asks if I thinks my own dad is watching me, and I say, Sure, yeah, maybe. Thinking: *Jesus, no, I hope not.* For both our sakes. Better to be in prison with Wes Abbot's dad, with TV and a cellmate.

He writes down whatever I say. He asks if I have any heroes, and I say, Sure, tons of them. Who? I think about it for a minute and finally tell him Margaret Thatcher. I have no idea why. He asks what I admire about her. Nothing, absolutely nothing comes to mind. His pen hovers over his legal pad.

Can I change my answer? I say.

Fifty miles south of us is Cape Canaveral, a primary Russian target in a nuclear attack. I imagine that when the bombs come we'll be instantly vaporized. I imagine it constantly. My mother urges me to write a letter to President Reagan, and I do. I ask him why he tested the microphone at a press conference by saying, *I've signed legislation to outlaw Russia forever. We begin bombing in five minutes.* Was he trying to be funny? I give it to my mother, thinking she'll throw it away or keep it in a shoebox somewhere, like a note to the tooth fairy. Later, I receive a letter and a signed picture of Ronald Reagan smiling atop a horse.

Nancy and I love receiving mail from children like you, he writes.

My sales catalog arrives. It turns out Captain O needs kids like me to sell Christmas cards and top-quality stationery and seasonal gifts. *Show your catalog to friends, relatives, neighbors*, the welcome letter says. *Anyone's a prospect! With Olympic you pay nothing, owe nothing, return nothing!*

My mother gamely browses the catalog and asks me to explain how it works again. I tell her about the sales army, the famous name prizes, the stereo system. It's just like a job, I say. She flips through the catalog for a long time, saddened by it, or tired, I can't tell. She picks a set of scalloped thank-you cards. One of our finest items, I say like a glib salesman. I think you'll be very happy with these. Please don't do that, she says, closing her eyes. How much do you have to sell for a stereo? she asks. One hundred and ninety items, I tell her. She sighs and gets up and pours herself a glass of wine, lights another cigarette, and sits down with the catalog in front of her. She opens it again and looks for something else to buy.

*   *   *

Our dog Linda dies almost exactly a year to the day after my father died. My mother pays a coworker to come take her away. He carries her out to his Jeep wrapped in a Hawaiian Tropic towel. Died of a broken heart, my mother tells everyone. I refuse to believe it. How can an obese poodle be experiencing something more keenly than I am? I beg for a new dog, one I can name and who likes people and who doesn't growl when I try to play with her. My mother buys me a turtle instead. I forget to feed it for a week and it dies too.

She tells me he could do unfathomable calculations in his head. She says that he liked reading me The Velveteen Rabbit. She says that horses could tell he was a good person. She says that I asked him if he was going to have to die to feel better. And when it was clear he wouldn't recover, he asked to speak to me alone in his hospital room. I don't remember. Maybe he did and maybe he didn't. His voice is barely audible, there's just a little bit of it left, and I have to lean in close to listen as he says goodbye and he loves me and he knows I'll grow into a remarkable person and it's unfair he can't be around to see it and whatever else dying fathers tell their only sons… she says he took my hand and wouldn't let go until it was time for me to leave, but if he and I were alone, how does she know?

* * *

She won't even drive past the hospital anymore. She takes the most convoluted routes to avoid it. Too painful for her, I think at first. Then I wonder if she's doing it for me.

I knock on ten doors in Lakebridge Estates with no answer. Finally a man comes to the door in a sleeveless shirt and nylon running shorts. He invites me inside, into the kitchen, where he points out a wall covered floor to ceiling with neatly stacked oatmeal canisters, and through the living room and onto his screened-in patio. He sits in a wicker chair, legs crossed, the shorts riding up on him, and I hand him the catalog. I have no sales pitch. I tell him that I'm trying to earn money for a school trip, which seems slightly more reputable than a stereo system. Where? he says, browsing the catalog. Holland, I say. Holland, he repeats. Red Light District. That's kind of a weird place to go for school, isn't it? He closes the catalog. Sorry, man, he says. I live on a fixed income. We sit there until I work up the nerve to ask for my catalog back. Want to see the upstairs? he asks as he's showing me out. I mumble no thanks and scurry home.

Later, when I tell friends about it, they're amazed I didn't take off running when he invited me inside. That dude was gonna chain you to his waterbed, Kyle says. Feed you fish sticks and make you his sex dwarf. I laugh along with them, but I'm uneasy at how stunted my sense of danger is. No inner alarm went off when I followed him inside. No voice told me to turn back, get out, go home. I was mostly just curious. Wondering idly, as I do when watching a cartoon or a game show, what happens next.

I remember years ago seeing a grainy photo of a teenage girl on the front page of the newspaper. This was before I could read, so I asked my mother what the story was about, and she skimmed it and said, She won a prize at school. For what? I asked. Her eyes were fixed on the girl's picture. For some vegetables she grew, she said finally, and she folded the newspaper and tucked it under her arm, but I could still see the doomed girl peeking out. I notice now like I didn't then how the seeds of future misfortune are hidden in photographs. Only in retrospect can they be detected.

In seventh grade, Mr. Withers brings a terrarium with an egg inside to class. He calls us to the front of the room and uses a special light to candle the speckled egg from below, illuminating a tangled knot of veins. Guess what's inside, he says. Some guess chick. Some guess robin. A few days later he candles it again, and we can discern four legs and a tail. When water starts to bead on the outside we gather around. While we wait for it to hatch he tells us bearded dragons are born with a single tooth. An egg tooth. They use it once to escape into the world, then it falls off and they swallow it.

What can we deduce from this? he asks. He never lets us be amazed—he spoils every moment with a lesson. Egg teeth, rainbows, alpenglow, jewel wasps. He has to name everything, bleed it of mystery by explaining what it is and what it means. Musical chairs is a lesson in supply and demand. The Smurfs are communists. He sees me looking at my sales catalog and asks what it is. I explain it to him, and he tells me to go to the P encyclopedia and look up *pyramid scheme*. For five minutes I stand at the bookshelf of encyclopedias reading about the ancient pyramids. In Egypt they were built west of the Nile so that once the pharaoh died, his soul could join the setting sun in the afterlife. They were designed to be resurrection machines.

So now you know, Mr. Withers says.

And knowing is half the battle, two kids say simultaneously. It's what GI Joe says at the end of the show when he tells you something you need to know.

My mother and I drive past a house covered in a red-and-blue-striped tent, and I ask her what's going on inside, and she says that it's a private circus. *A private circus*. I believe her. I know very little about what goes on in other people's houses. I can imagine clowns in the guest bathroom, bears in the Florida room, delights withheld from me behind red-and-blue canvas. A lovely image, but soon enough I'll have to pull all the lies out like stingers. Even the loveliest will leave a mark. Whenever she burns dinner, she serves it anyway and says it's better for us.

Years later, talking to her on the phone, she tells me I'm mistaken about a few things. We didn't move to a new town house after he died. She says we lived in that gravy-brown town house for years. He painted the whale mural on the wall for you, she says. And he's the one who smoked menthol cigarettes. She doesn't remember any wildfires. But she remembers the boy who was abducted down in Hialeah. What's-his-name.

Adam Walsh, I say.

Poor kid, she says.

He went missing from Sears. We all combed the pinewoods near our house until his body was found in a culvert. The newspaper republished the picture of him, angelic in his baseball cap. His parents cried on the nightly news, and my mother cried with them. I slept with a light on.

When I ask about the faux-leather recliner, she says, Yep, they took it with them.

I never saw it in their house, I say.

Who knows. It was a long time ago. I hated that chair.

She and I take turns playing I remember. I remember our Nissan Pulsar. She remembers the Bicentennial. I remember owls in our backyard. She remembers Sensei Duane.

Sensei Duane. How could I have forgotten him? She met him at a Parents Without Partners meeting. At first she thought he was hitting on her, but it turned out he was recruiting boys for his martial arts dojo. At River of Tradition we teach the four pillars of respect, he said, pointing to the patch on his coat, where the pillars were listed. She wasn't wearing her glasses, but it looked like one of them was *custard*.

Your son's at an age where he should be working hard on his belief system, Sensei Duane said, though she'd never told him how old I was.

Me and five other fatherless boys sitting cross-legged on reeking dojo mats. Sensei Duane, short, red haired, waterlogged looking, sketching the sad details of our future if we continue down the path we're on.

Worse than you can imagine, he says. Some of y'all are dead. Those are the lucky ones. The rest of you are like those lobsters in fish tanks pretending you're still part of the animal kingdom. You got no idea how helpless you are.

At thirteen I can't imagine a time when I don't know exactly how helpless I am. I can imagine a hundred futures for myself, and none at all. How karate figures into it I cannot say, but Sensei Duane's lessons don't include much karate. Measure twice, cut once, he tells us. He measures and measures and measures.

His lessons all begin the same way: The thing you must remember…

The thing you must remember is posture. The thing you must remember is you're a window. The thing you must remember is to never challenge a blind man to a seeing contest.

He keeps a detailed notebook on each of his disciples. That's what he says. If we finish three years of training, he'll give us the notebook as a reward. It'll be like living in a studio apartment all our lives and then being handed a key to rooms we never knew existed. I imagine him in his office after I leave, jotting down observations. Noticing me, assessing my potential, charting courses around my limitations and all the things that scare me and shouldn't, the things that don't and should, away from the helpless future that awaits me.

You aren't becoming anything, he says. You *are* something. And my job is to help you wake it up.

I like the sound of that. As if some better version of myself is snoozing nearby, and someone just has to nudge it awake.

I keep thinking about the seeing contest. I wonder if it works like a vision test at the doctor's. Are there prizes? How would a blind man beat me?

I clear out space on the bookshelves in my room and move a beanbag chair in front of where the speakers will be. For now my tape player sits there. I've made a recording of Hungry Like the Wolf and listened to it about eighty times. I've just figured out it's about sex, not wolves. I turn up the volume until I can hear my nasally breathing on the recording. My mother sneezed downstairs between *mouth is alive* and *running inside* so now that's part of the song too. I close my eyes and imagine everything clearer, truer, bigger. The song ends, and I rewind it and play it again.

After school I take my sales catalog to the Trails, a subdivision of houses along the river. I ride my skateboard, a delaminated Nash Nuke Baby I found abandoned near my house. Cars honk as they pass, drivers scream epithets at me and flip me off. For some reason the sight of a kid on a skateboard infuriates them. My balance is improving but I'm still wobbly. My center of gravity shifts without warning. Just past the entrance I bend my knees atop a mellow hill and feel the simple thrill of movement as I gain speed. One of my front wheels catches a mulch chip near the bottom, and I fall on my hip and scrape my elbow. The catalog goes flying into the street. No one sees me and I'm not hurt, so I stay on the ground. If I wanted to I could start crying right now—it might feel good to cry, cathartic. I wait to see if I want to.

The houses in the Trails are sprawling and hidden among citrus trees and oleander bushes and gnarled oaks. People answer their doors here. I've rehearsed a slightly more believable story about raising money for school chorus. We're going to perform at Epcot Center, the amusement park of the future. Sometimes I'm invited inside, never past the foyer. All the houses in the Trails have foyers. And eat-in kitchens and stairwell walls covered with framed photographs. A woman holding a weary dachshund quickly scans the catalog and buys two sets of Christmas cards. Her neighbor orders a desk organizer. The woman two doors down buys jasmine candles. She points to my elbow, tells me I'm bleeding. She goes into the bathroom and brings back antiseptic to spray over the scrape. It foams and stings and the woman regards me with undisguised pity, which is fine. I can live with pity. Then the front door opens behind me and a girl from school walks in. Bethany Blythe, one of those names bestowed by the heavens to popular girls. There's a skateboard in our driveway, she says as I step aside to let her through. She glances at me, gleans everything she needs to know in an instant, then looks at her mom. Complex messages pass between them.

He's in chorus too, the woman says.

Bethany scrutinizes me again. No, he's not, she says. He's... a grub.

The woman gasps with indignation but Bethany assures her it's okay. That's what they call themselves, she says to me. Right?

I say yes, though I've never heard the word in my life.

She heads upstairs. Her mother watches her go. Bethany's been peevish since her ballet teacher died, she says as she's filling out the check.

By the end of the day, I've knocked on every door in the Trails. I count my order sheet: nineteen sales. The most successful day imaginable, and I'm now eligible for a latch hook set or the zipper carry-all bag. If I sell five more items, the Hot Numbers solar calculator will be mine. I've exhausted the Trails, given up on Lakebridge Estates, and my mother has ordered everything she can afford. She suggests that I try my teachers or my friends' parents, and the speed with which I shoot down the idea confirms the fact that I'm doing something shameful, something best kept hidden.

I start middle school across the street from the beach, my mother's alma mater. Our mascot is the sand crab. On certain days when the classroom windows are open you can hear waves faintly pounding. The history teacher shows slides from his summer trip to Costa Rica. We watch Pink Floyd's The Wall in psychology class. Other teachers openly flirt with girls in the halls. After school my friends and I skate the loading dock behind Publix. I learn to ollie. I learn to roll on the ground when I fall. I am brave and dumb—I fall more than anyone else. I purposely fail an English placement test and end up in a class with second-language speakers. For months we practice prepositions and subject-verb agreement, and I work hard, harder than I ever have, memorizing what I already know to become what I already am, until the school realizes what happened and moves me to a different class.

* * *

A moment of silence for Adam Walsh before the jokes arrive. Did you know he had dandruff? They found his Head & Shoulders in the canal. If you laugh, then you'll hear the next one. If you don't laugh, you'll still hear the next one. What's better than a hundred dead babies stapled to a tree? One dead baby stapled to a hundred trees. Nothing off-limits. Nothing unthinkable.

In math class a woman with a kind face explains that she'll be filling in for Mr. Gray while he recovers from having a pig valve grafted to his heart. She says algebra is the science of restoring what's missing. It is the reunion of broken parts. After we finish doing practice problems from the textbook, she tells us about historical figures who were interred far from where their severed parts—arms and legs and, in one case, nose—were buried. Every day a different figure: Tycho Brahe, Stonewall Jackson, Frida Kahlo. She keeps the whole class riveted. When the bell rings no one moves.

A week later a flushed and snuffling Mr. Gray returns to class with his swine heart. His brush with death has taught him nothing of the deeper mysteries. He tells us the simplest solution is usually the correct one, which is neither interesting nor true, and when a kid asks if he ever thinks about the pig who died so that he could continue living, Mr. Gray says pigs are not *who*s, they are *that*s—and he does not. In class it's all we think about. That poor martyred pig floating in limbo, waiting for his broken part to be buried along with Mr. Gray, who at the very least could try to remember the pig's sacrifice from time to time. It's not like we're asking him to build a shrine for it.

All of us in class take turns oinking softly while he solves problems on the overhead projector, doing our best to help him not forget.

The orders arrive from Olympic Sales Club. *A first-time customer is a potential repeat customer!* Captain O says. I make my deliveries to people who can't remember what they ordered. One woman is surprised to see me again. I thought it was a scam, she says. Why'd she go along with it? I wonder. And quickly answer my own question: She was paying me to go away.

I never make another sale. I quit knocking on doors and give up on the stereo. When a catalog arrives I throw it away without opening it. I retire at twenty-seven sales, enough for a home-battery charger or a Type-Right typing tutor. Or I have the option of cashing out for $13.50, which is what I do. I buy an orange skid plate for my skateboard and five dollars' worth of stickers. I recalibrate, wait for the wanting to ebb, and wait.

For years I was a grub without knowing it. Grubbing around, thinking I was part of the animal kingdom. It's a perfect epithet, no wondering in it at all. I nod to my fellow grubs in the halls between classes. Math grubs. Future-farmer grubs. Girl grubs. Heavy-metal grubs. Thirteen-year-old grubs with incomprehensible mustaches. Now that I know what I am, I embrace it. I wear oversized Sansabelt slacks, the kind my father wore, and cut them off into shorts in warmer weather. A friend screen-prints the Rat Bones logo onto thrift-store shirts, and I wear those to school every day. We give each other haircuts and skate to school and sit through first period dirty and sweating and eat lunch out of plastic bread bags by the smokers' tree. One day the kids in PE class make me race Dale Hebert, whose left foot is encased in a plastic boot from a football injury. A hundred-yard dash. I barely win and everyone in class, even Coach Wakefield, lets out a big cheer afterward. I'm not sure whether they're cheering for Dale or me. I resolve to never run again. Beyond that, middle school is oddly tolerable. My fellow grubs and I, we laugh a lot, mostly at other people, rarely at ourselves.

I hear you're really into skateboarding, the school counselor says. It's great to have a passion at your age. He and I both agree that I'm very passionate.

He encourages my mother to find me positive male role models. How else will I become versed in the delicate art of manhood? Bryce, my cabin leader at a camp in the Everglades, tells me and the other boys Bible stories about himself. His favorite is the one where he comes home drunk to find an intruder in his house. The intruder, it turns out, was actually Satan—a kid asks how he could tell it was Satan, and Bryce points to his head and says, His horns. He says it so solemnly no one but me dares laugh. He and Satan wrestled all through the house, up the stairs, knocking pictures off the wall. They fought for hours, until Bryce accepted Christ as Lord and Savior. Satan was cast out of Bryce's hallway and back to hell. Now Bryce has SMP, Sober Mind Power, and isn't afraid of anyone. Do we want the kind of strength that can defeat a wrathful demon? He waits. The question isn't rhetorical. We all say yes.

Well then, we just have to do what he did.

Fight Satan? I ask, excited.

Accept Christ, he says.

Mr. Staller says that when he was my age, he could already speak Latin. He says he hasn't lost a game of Scrabble in twelve and a half years. His classroom has a world map with orange pins sticking out of all the countries he's visited. He nominates me for the Society for Excellence, some after-school club he advises, but I never join. I have no use for society, or excellence. All I want is to silently vanquish my enemies. And to have enemies worth silently vanquishing. I wish Satan would come to my house. I buy a blowgun from the flea market, seven dollars of my own money, and bring it home: a plastic flute with one sad dart. In the woods behind my house, I aim it at a tree, but

I can never blow hard enough for the dart to stick to anything, not even the ground.

One night I wake up next to my mother on my father's side of the bed. I have no memory of coming into her room. I lie very still and watch car-light shadows rove from wall to ceiling to wall. She sleeps with her back to me and snores with grinding constancy, as if some terrible snarl trapped inside her is coming out in increments. He can't, she mumbles.

He can't what? I whisper to her, and wait for her to reveal news too devastating to tell me during the day.

He won't need any, she says.

He won't need any what? I say, nudging her. She won't answer.

I wake up next to her often, somehow teleported there during the night. She starts locking her door, and I wake up on the hard rug outside her room like a banished pet.

You're getting too old to sleep with me, she says one morning. I know that. Of course I know that. How can I tell her I don't even remember moving from my bed to hers? It seems worse somehow, more aberrant.

A book appears on my dresser with the title Where Did I Come From? There's a naked, confused-looking baby on the cover.

This book is all about you, it begins. *We wrote it because we thought you'd like to know exactly where you came from.*

I don't care to know exactly where I came from. The book's sudden appearance disheartens me. I hide it from my mother, never suspecting that she's the one who left it there. *Making love*, the book says, *is a very nice feeling for the man and the woman. If you can imagine a gentle tickle that starts in your stomach and spreads all over, that will give you some idea of what it's like.*

Onto the shelf it goes, next to When Bad Things Happen to Good People. Birth and death, with nothing in between. I quit going into her room, quit looking to her for solace at night.

In English class we discuss The Scarlet Letter and Silas Marner. I haven't read a word of either one. The only books I willingly read are collections of Ripley's Believe It or Not! cartoons, full of hand-drawn illustrations and accompanying captions. A woman in Leipzig who once ate a bicycle piece by piece. A man in Tashkent who can blow out candles with air from his eyeballs. I read them until the oddities become certainties, crucial, immutable, curiously soothing. There are no lessons. Nothing is demanded of me beyond a simple choice: to believe or not.

I sleep over at Manav's house and his father wakes us at three in the morning to watch Halley's Comet. We sit on cabana chairs in the driveway, his father sipping from a mug of Bailey's and me and Manav shivering and anticipating the moment the comet will scream across the atmosphere, spraying shards of fire and dust and ice. The stars pulse. An hour passes. The moon hangs there, dumb as always.

He wakes us again at dawn and points to a faint blue scribble in the sky. Barely scratched us, he says. He hands us each a chunk of charcoal, freezing cold. I found this in the front yard, he says. I hold it to my nose. Charred rock, a molar plucked from the jaw of an old god. I put it in the side pocket of my backpack and forget about it for months—by the time I remember it the chunk is lost, dust.

At Manav's house: snacks in the pantry, video-game console in the living room, trampoline in the backyard, fifty albums in his bedroom. I'm drawn to the meal chart on the refrigerator. A color-coded menu for each day of the week with an assigned cook: Manav, his sister and brother, and his parents take turns making food for the family. Reading it leaves a bitter feeling akin to jealousy smeared through with self-pity. Manav says he hates how predictable his days are and wishes he could be like me, free to roam. We sit on his bedroom floor listening to albums. He buys one a week with his allowance, usually whatever the record-store cashier girl, whom we're both in love with, recommends. I read along with the lyrics on the album sleeves—what I'm hearing is far more interesting than what they're singing. He makes tapes of them for me to listen to in my room. I skate home from his house imagining the conversations he and his father have about me.

Days pass, a certain aimlessness abides. My breakfast cereal provides 100 percent nutrition for the day, but the grayer mysteries remain unsolved. I once had a picture book called What Do People Do All Day? Either the book never answered the question, or I've forgotten. Sometimes I fall asleep to the sound of my mother talking to friends on the telephone. When she's been drinking Gallo wine her voice gets so happy, almost lifelike. I can't make out what she's saying, but I carry the giddy murmur of her voice into sleep with me, enfold myself in it like a fortune inside a cookie. Certain secrets, I know, will reveal themselves soon. I want to get it over with. I can feel time like a tide rising and falling but never running out, never as a thing I'll one day have to portion out and struggle against.

My mother starts taking me to church on Sundays. She says we're Methodists now.

During the week she comes home late from the community college and doesn't eat dinner. She pours herself a glass of wine with ice, asks how my day was. She makes lesson plans at the dining room table—she's studying to be an elementary school teacher. She drinks too much and worries constantly about money. We are poor now. Maybe we always were.

She asks so little of me but I still have a hard time giving it to her. Sometimes I hear her sigh when she hears me coming down the stairs in the morning. We argue constantly. She wants me to be less demanding. I want her to be like my friends' moms. Cheerful, happy, interested, benign. She's kindest when I'm sick. My inner light dimmed slightly, my needs basic and discernible. She buys magazines for me to read in bed, then warms some cream of mushroom and pours bacon bits over it. I like it when she flattens her palm on my forehead to check for a fever. It's the only time I can recall her showing me physical affection, using her hand to measure me, waiting, and withdrawing it with her diagnosis.

I overhear her telling Bunny that she's considering taking out a personals ad in the newspaper. Bunny is ecstatic, frothing with advice: Don't use your real name, she says, don't reveal more than you have to, don't use the word *companionship*. I'm not entirely clear about what a personals ad is but I can guess. She's going to put herself up for grabs like a litter of Chihuahuas in the PennySaver. You're a catch, Bunny tells her. Are you listening? There's no reason you should be alone. I wait for her to correct Bunny. She's not alone. She has me. We have each other. I wait.

* * *

Watching TV one afternoon I notice the adding machine is missing from the shelf. I go to the closet and my father's powder-blue cardigan is still there, sheathed in dry-cleaner plastic.

Sometimes I think about those scraps of paper he wrote on. I wonder where they went. Just before he died, he'd lose his voice for days and write me dozens of little notes, laboring over every letter of every word. I read them slowly, embarrassed by the whole transaction. By the time I looked up he'd already be working on the next one. Maybe my grandmother packed them away too. It's probably best they're gone, but I do wonder about them. Some were things he would've said to me if he could have—*Feeling better today. Doubleheader later*—some he said only because he couldn't.

I skate around town with friends, a few dollars in my pocket and no discernible plan. One of us buys lunch at an all-you-can-eat buffet and we take turns eating from the same plate. We bomb the biggest hill in town, a high bridge over the intracoastal river, and I get speed wobbles. I'm hucked into the air and I tumble and skid ten feet across ridged asphalt. My friend Tom says the only thing to do is walk into the ocean and let salt water cleanse the wounds. It sounds reasonable enough. I limp over the sand dunes, leave my shoes and shirt in the sea oats, and wade into the burning water.

School ends and I take a Greyhound bus to Kentucky to visit my aunt and grandmother. A twenty-five-hour ride. A foul odyssey. In Florida the man next to me repeatedly reaches into his waistband to pluck something from his crotch, kill it with his thumbnail, and drop it onto the floor. I tuck the cuffs of my pants into my socks, just in case. In Georgia a man tries to lure me into the bathroom to buy his Starter jacket for ten dollars. I'm burning *up* in this, he says. I tell him I don't need a Starter jacket. How about an earring? he says, pointing to his ear, earringless. By Tennessee everyone's drunk, singing, laughing, snoring.

A guy across the aisle coughs a nineteenth-century cough. I turn to him and he grins and whispers, Looks like I caught a little mousey. His hands are cupped over his lap. He opens them and before I can turn away, there's his penis, gray and torpid like something stillborn. He coughs, fills the air between us with sweet floral rot.

I shut my eyes for the rest of the trip. I remember reading an article about a teacher arrested for lewd and lascivious conduct. It said that after getting a personal body part stuck in a park bench, he needed some bystanders to help him free it. Such a strange expression: *personal body part*. Aren't all body parts personal? When I debark in Louisville the man across the aisle calls out, Say bye. Say bye. I'm not sure whether he's talking to me or to his penis.

My grandmother and aunt meet me outside the bus station. They ask me how my trip was, ask what I want to do while I'm there. They don't ask about my mother. I talk about her anyway. I tell them we've been going to church lately. I think they'll like that. They want to know what kind of church. Methodist, I tell them. Silence, not even a courtesy nod. Or maybe Episcopalian? I say.

They live in a big brick colonial filled with antiques. We walk through and they point out a Dickens-era Christmas village on display in the sitting room seven months after Christmas. Cross-stitched Bible verses framed on the wall. I don't see the faux-leather recliner anywhere. In the kitchen: bowls of fruit on the counter. In the basement: my father's golf clubs against the wall, gathering dust. Finally, his old room. His bed with a quilt my grandmother made. His closet and dresser filled with his clothes. On the nightstand, black-and-white pictures of him in basketball poses wearing a Kentucky jersey. I ask if he played in college.

For Adolph Rupp, my aunt says. You didn't know that? He was a star.

I only knew he fell in love with horses and numbers. My mother rarely talks about his life before they met. Once she showed me a photo of him and her at the beach and told me she could pinpoint the exact day and knew it was the happiest of her life because that was the day they got engaged.

My aunt says they used to take a bus to Lexington to watch games until he got tired of playing for Rupp and transferred to a little nothing college in Florida and broke a bunch of scoring records, worked at the track, and met my mother.

We watch Wheel of Fortune but not Jeopardy. Trebek's too cocky, they say, acting like he's the one who invented the questions. I'm in bed before sundown, sealed in a museum. He is closer to me here and more distant. I fall asleep paging through his high school yearbook. All those cryptic inscriptions and reverent haircuts.

Three meals a day at the dining room table. Big country breakfast, big country lunch, big country dinner. Big country dessert. Eating is an event requiring discipline, intuition, endurance. One must ask the person closest to the milk gravy to please pass the milk gravy. One must never place his elbows on the table. One must refer to deviled eggs as dressed eggs so as not to invite the devil into the house. One must pause to say grace before eating without saying anything aloud and release an *amen* at the proper time. No one ever has explained the mechanics of prayer to me, so I treat it like a wish list, closing my eyes to tell God everything I want. I don't know what's expected of me in return. The only thing I hear in church that rings true is the idea that I was born incomplete and that my natural inclinations are faulty, damnable even. Sometimes we talk about dinner while eating breakfast.

Before he got sick my father visited them twice a year without my mother and me. I've been here once, when I was eleven months old. The only exceptional things about me then were that I could swim before I could walk and I drank Tang straight from the bottle. The astronauts drank it, my mother would say whenever pressed about feeding a toddler sugar water. That neon-orange space powder rotted my baby teeth to the root. I had a mouth full of brown teeth for years. My grandmother asks if my mother still feeds me Tang, and I say she no longer feeds me anything, meaning I'm old enough to feed myself, but it sounds like an accusation. I feel vaguely like I need to assert something about myself and my mother here, but I don't know what. The two of them are judgmental, self-satisfied, full of prejudice. They say things like *It's the children I feel sorry for* when they see an interracial couple. They direct all kinds of epithets I've never heard before to the TV. I sigh and shake my head but it will be years before I'm confident enough to challenge them. I bring my mother up whenever I can. I say she bought a used Nissan Pulsar. She's studying for a certification, I tell them. She's going to be an elementary school teacher.

Well, that's news to me, my grandmother says. I didn't know she even liked kids. Remember when she dropped you off at school on a teacher-duty day and you had to hang out with the Black janitor while she went shopping for hours?

He was nice, I say. He taught me how to mop, I say. They laugh and laugh.

No mother should outlive her child, my aunt tells me while my grandmother's at church. She's at church four days a week, knitting, eating, singing, praying. It's unnatural what happened to her, she says. I never reply, How about a nine-year-old kid losing his father? I don't even think it. We sit in solemn silence for my grandmother's loss.

A cousin I've never met takes me to lunch. His name's Rusty. We have the same last name and I feel strange around him, as if we share an incriminating secret. He drives a Buick with a cooler full of beers in the trunk. He turns on the radio and asks what kind of music I like. Below the radio are five punch buttons with a single letter etched on them: B-U-I-C-K. He's rearranged them to read C-I-K-U-B. When I ask why, he points to each one: Can. I. Kiss. U. Baby.

He says my aunt's probably a closeted lezzy. He says he once saw my dad dunk on a regulation rim, like a year before he died. Your dad loved Ford Mustangs, Rusty says. I like the way he refers to him as *your dad*. We go to Wendy's. A sign on the drive-thru window says, CONDIMENTS AVAILABLE UPON REQUEST. I don't know what condiments are so I ask Rusty. Something you wear during sex, he tells me, so the woman doesn't get pregnant.

On the drive home I sense he wants to tell me something. Parked in front of my aunt and grandmother's house, he finally says, So the thing about your dad... and you might not know this because you were young when he died, but he was extremely well-endowed. You know what I mean, right? That man was blessed with the family unit. Rusty sighs a mournful sigh, then adds, I was too. Fortunately. So, he says. He looks at me and waits.

I say, Okay, nice seeing you, thanks, and try to squirm out of the car.

I guess it's something in our blood, he says.

I remember visiting the horse track he managed, how exotic it seemed. Six, seven years old, walking around with him as he greeted groundskeepers and jockeys, naming horses as we went through the stables, and me feeling, probably for the first time, proud. Lucky. Knowing the source but not the name of the feeling.

* * *

My grandmother drives me to the mall and calmly insists I get my hair cut. It's too long in the back, she says. I run my hand along my neck where there's maybe an inch of hair. You need to look presentable, she says. She tells the barber to give me a high and tight, which doesn't sound good at all and is worse than it sounds. I come away shorn, powdered, my head looking like a massive diseased pumpkin. As a reward she takes me to a department store and buys me three button-up oxford shirts, two pairs of pleated slacks, a belt, and a teal velour sweater with my initials stitched in elaborate cursive on the breast pocket. She must have ordered it ahead of time. I am comforted for fifteen minutes by the thought that I'll never have to actually wear these clothes, until our final stop, a photography studio, where my grandmother tells me to go into the bathroom and change into them. I pose in front of seasonal backdrops while the photographer tells me to smile more genuinely, more radiantly. What are your hobbies? she asks. Deep-sea fishing, I say. I didn't know that, my grandmother says. Think about deep-sea fishing, the photographer says. When that doesn't work: Think about a girl you like. Think about a birthday party. I change the second we get home.

I buy a postcard to send to my mother with nothing written on it except our address. You have to write a message, my aunt says when I ask her to send it. Don't you know how postcards work?

* * *

I stay with them for a month. We go to church four times. I'm the oldest kid in Sunday school by at least three years. The teacher hands out paper and crayons and tells us to sketch what we think God looks like, an exercise with the cheerless whiff of a lesson, so I ignore it. Instead, while other kids draw their bearded wizards, I draw my home state, the state of Florida. I add highways and rivers and lakes, put a star in the panhandle for the capital. The teacher walks around, offering encouragement. By the time he gets to me I'm finished, ready to be chastised. He asks if I drew it from memory and I say yes and he picks it up and looks more closely. At last he sets it down and says, You didn't understand the assignment. But your coastlines are perfect.

Is your mother dating? my aunt asks. I tell her no, and my aunt says, She should be. People remarry all the time. In my case, I'm waiting to meet a man as smart as me. What if a man as smart as you doesn't want to date you? I ask. His loss, she says.

She asks if I remember begging my father to take me back to the magic store. He had no clue what you were talking about, she says. There never was any magic store.

Sparrows perch atop headstones in the family burial plot. A screech of insects, then a wider screech in a distant field— slowly the screeches merge. My aunt and grandmother pull weeds. I am here to feel certain things. It's miserably hot out and a bee is shadowing me because it knows I'm an intruder and his tombstone is so new it looks like a novelty tombstone. A Halloween decoration. I'm surprised to see my mother's name next to his, her final date unwritten. Like an invitation to a party that begins at eight and ends at question mark. It seems ominous and strange. Was it cheaper to have her name engraved alongside his?

I sidestep the graves and try to remember the names: Mayme, Squire, Jouett.

No need trying to avoid them, my grandmother says. No one can hurt them where they are.

I never doubted he was gone but now I have proof. We stop for frozen yogurt on the way home and abolish it silently in the car.

I pack one of the T-shirts from his dresser into my duffel bag. BETCHA LOVE US!, it says, the slogan of the horse track he managed. It doesn't seem like a transgression until I ask my grandmother if I can have his picture from the nightstand and she says, No, not yet. Not yet? When we die, my aunt says, it's all yours. She's not joking. As a parting gift they give me a Samsonite briefcase with his initials on the latches. I sit with it in my lap on the bus back to Florida. I'll never use it. I am certain of that. In college I will keep it in the trunk of my car, and one day I'll walk out to find the car rear-ended in its parking place. Before it's towed, I will pay a guy to pry the briefcase out of the trunk. It will take an hour and cost two hundred dollars, but the briefcase will emerge unharmed. Feels empty, the guy will say as he hands it to me. It is, it was. On the bus back to Florida the man next to me asks if I've seen the commercial with the gorilla and the suitcase and I say, Oh, yeah. I don't know what he's talking about, but I'm trying to master the sort of vigorous agreement that puts an end to conversation. He keeps talking. Somehow the subject of my father comes up, and he says, Depending on who you throw in with, your old man's in a better place, a worse place, or in-between places. He offers me his bag of sunflower seeds. When the driver announces we've entered Florida, the man lifts his ass toward me and releases a wet, rueful fart.

While I've been gone our town house has developed a curious, sexual odor and my mother is acting cagey. I complain about my aunt and grandmother, and she has nothing to say except: They're doing their best. She won't share my outrage about their refusal to give me the picture. On the kitchen table are dozens of paper sacks and inside each are aspirin, mouthwash, tampons, wet wipes. For the homeless, she says. She's joined a new church that encourages good works. She's been cruising A1A looking for people to give the bags to, but she can't figure out who is and isn't homeless. Everyone by the beach looks a little homeless. She's managed to give away just three of the fifty kits she made. We've been driving around, she tells me, and saying to people, *Pardon me, but are you down on your luck?*

We? I say.

Years later, I call to ask her the name of the man she started dating when I went to Kentucky, and she says, Are you sure you got the timing right? I'm sure. Well, Ed is the only man I dated. And we didn't really date. I won't argue with her. But she did date him. They went to dinner, the movies, the dog track. Once he took me to a magic show.

Your dad's birthday is Saturday, she says, changing the subject. He'd be eighty-one. Here's what I wonder, she says. Here's what's been bugging me lately. Do you think he'd be dead by now if he didn't already die?

No one can silence me like my mother. It's a powerful gift, probably developed back when I was agitated on my leash in her womb.

Where were we? she says after a while. She often repeats this phrase on the phone. Now where were we? As if conversation is a punishing labyrinth we're navigating together. Careful not to lose our way, careful to measure where we're going against where we've been. Oh, now I remember, she says. I was about to tell you about the animal sounds coming from the roof. I thought something was trying to claw its way in—turns out something was trying to claw its way *out*...

* * *

Ed says he trains elephants at Circus World. I don't believe him. If he worked around elephants he'd be wiser, more dignified. He plays the banjo. He likes to whistle. He's eager to win me over but he's an inept army. He doesn't know when to retreat and when to advance. He'll declare an enthusiasm, then try to march me to it: Look at that sunset, all those oranges and blues; hey, listen to these sweet guitar licks by this band you've never heard of from Cocoa Beach; try a bite of this tangelo from my tangelo tree, I rub rancid honey on the trunk, which is why they're so delicious.

In the future whenever I read about an elephant trampling circus-goers I'll think about Ed. His acne scars and battleship hats and transition lenses that never seem to fully untint. He drives a midnight-blue conversion van. He gave me a tour of it the day we met. A normal van has one, maybe two ashtrays; his conversion van has five. A normal van has a tape deck; his has a tape deck and TV set. A normal van has normal seats called *seats*; his van has wider, plusher seats called *captain's seats*.

I know it's selfish, I know it's unfair, but the idea of her enjoying herself with him infuriates me. When she's out late I wait for her in the kitchen, sincere and vital as a lighthouse keeper.

Rooting through my mother's closet I find a mauve dildo, precisely the punishment a boy merits for rooting through his mother's closet.

* * *

Ed buys her a charm bracelet, which she wears when they're together. One of the charms is a miniature square cage holding a meticulously folded five-dollar bill, and I free it one afternoon with tweezers, unfold it, and use it to buy a Circle Jerks cassette from the scornful cashier girl at Atlantic Sounds. She wears her hair in a Chelsea cut—short bangs and two wispy forelocks—and combat boots with yellow laces to signal she isn't racist. Red laces mean racist, yellow laces mean not racist, white and black laces mean something else. She makes me show her my money before she'll talk to me—once I do she's helpful, friendly even, and I buy whatever she tells me to buy. Sometimes reggae, sometimes rockabilly, sometimes songs without a single decipherable lyric, just berserk guitars and singers gargling bile. I come home to find my mother at the kitchen table trying to fold a five-dollar bill. She doesn't look up when I walk in. I knew the moment I'd unfolded it, how painstakingly accordioned it was, that only an origami master could pack a new bill into that cage. It doesn't stop her from struggling for hours to undo what I've done, sighing, waiting for an apology. Finally she gives up and goes to the hardware store and buys a dead bolts for her bedroom. I lie on my carpet listening to music, dream of the cashier thawing with every passing song. Instead of saying sweet dreams my mother bolts her lock to sign off for the night.

* * *

The chemistry teacher sends me and Daryl to the vice-principal for disrupting class. We're past our final warning and our punishment is four licks with Hammerhead, the paddle hanging on his wall. Its face is the size of an oar, a grinning shark on it like on an old bomber plane.

First he has to get permission. He calls Daryl's mom. She says, What? Nope, no way. We hear her through the receiver. He calls mine. She doesn't even hesitate. You have my blessing, she says, as if ordaining it from on high. The vice-principal grunts as he swings the paddle, pausing to let each lick resonate.

Alone in his hospital room after saying goodbye to me, where do his thoughts take him? Is he afraid? Relieved? Did he say all he wanted to? What nags me is the likelihood something crucial went unsaid. Alone in my bed, unsleeping, I imagine him alone in his. He waits. Readies himself, empties himself. My mother says he used to visualize a round of golf when he couldn't sleep, working his way through the course shot by shot, hole by hole. Maybe this sustains him for a while. How much longer did he have to wait? Two days is unimaginable, eight hours, even a half hour, unimaginable.

* * *

In a baseball field with my classmates we look into the southern sky and wait for the Challenger launch, follow the orange streak as it rises and then bursts into white plumes like I always suspected it would. Inside the teacher turns on the TV to confirm what we know: It has exploded. I prepare for the next catastrophe. I wait for tropical depressions to become hurricanes. I dream of nuclear winter. I follow serial killers on the news, read about them in the newspaper. There's one in every town. The Damsel of Death and her big beseeching eyes, she's ours. She murders men along the interstate west of town, shoots them point-blank and steals their cars. She's finally apprehended at a biker bar near my house. Killers. I feel their presence as tangibly as any god or overseer. Where I'll be and where I've been: an archipelago of crime scenes. Wandering the woods behind my house I find a single ankle sock, a frayed length of rope, and I know I'm about to stumble upon something brutal, something unspeakable.

Ed comes to the house with a box of old stereo equipment. A Unisonic 100 dual cassette tape deck with RadioShack speakers. My mother stands at my doorway as he sets it up. I feel an odd smear of impatience, gratitude, sadness, resentment. I keep it to myself. If I tell her I don't want it she won't understand. She'll think it's because it's not as nice as the one I wanted.

When he's done he plays one of my tapes, the Exploited screaming *punk's not dead*. Whoa, he says, peeking in at the label. I like it. He names a few bands that he thinks I'd like.

I look at my mother, who mouths *say thank you*. I thank him.

A few days later he takes me to see the magician David Copperfield, just the two of us. Our seats are in the third row. David Copperfield levitates over the audience and peers down at me and nods and I nod back. Ed keeps looking over to make sure I'm enjoying myself—I am, but my face stays rigid. David Copperfield has a beautiful redheaded assistant. He transports her to the Hoover Dam. She brings an audience member's herringbone necklace with her and holds it up on a video feed atop the dam. On the way home we go through each trick and try to figure out how it's done. When he pulls in front of our town house, I thank him and we shake hands like we've closed a deal. Then he says something about my father, earnest and sympathetic and rehearsed sounding, and instantly whatever good cheer I feel goes ice-cold.

A manila envelope, postmarked from Kentucky: PHOTOS: DO NOT BEND. It's his picture from the nightstand, I think. And some others by the feel of it. I rip open the envelope and pull out a half-dozen identical portraits of me in my monogrammed sweater. Autumnal scene, dipshit smirk, vacant eyes, doomed as a missing person.

Whose little boy are you? she used to say when she was tired of me. Scanning my face without recognition, a menu of foods she doesn't want in a language she doesn't speak. Shouldn't you go look for your mommy?

I hated that. When I remind her about it she acts like she doesn't remember. I bring it up more often than I should. At least I never drowned you in a bathtub, she says.

I remember certain words filling me with dread. Toothpick. That was one. Scissors. Struggling to sit still and feeling, deep in my torso, contrary urges zigzagging through me. Feeling like an ant mound about to be stomped open.

They spend Friday night at the Ocean Deck watching Windjammer, a local reggae band. I sit around and stew. I retrieve the dildo from her closet and place it vertically in the center of the foyer, where she and Ed will pass when they return. I'm not sure what my endgame is, whether it's a protest, a penalty, an art installation. They pull up. I listen. They open the front door and pause at the threshold.

* * *

How unfair, that childhood should drift further away as you age, and closer. What I miss most, I think, are the feelings of awe and consequence. Awe at all there was left to discover of the world's cryptic inner machinery, and the consequence of discovering it. Trent moves to town from California, bringing news of a brighter place. He wears hoop earrings and makes music on a four-track recorder in his room, plays all the instruments himself. He steals from snack machines. He attaches a long piece of packing tape to the edge of a dollar, creating a foot-and-a-half-long bill. Hold the tape while you insert it into a snack machine, pick what you want, wait until the machine tries to pull it in, then yank it out. Just a flick of the wrist. In ten minutes you've got forty bags of chips and fifteen dollars in change. He says when he flew here from California he smelled something awful when he stepped out of the airport, and the smell hasn't gone away.

My mother takes her first-grade students to Blue Springs to visit their class manatee, Karl. For months they've written him letters. At the springs, the guide points to a listless herd of manatees, ancient as dinosaur eggs in the clear water, and asks which is theirs. My mother tells him and the guide frowns and says, Oh, I'm sorry. Karl died last weekend.

    He says it with such enthusiasm she thinks he's joking. He goes on about industrial contaminants and the delicate ecosystem of the spring. A girl reaches for my mother's hand and holds it. When it becomes clear that they're just going to hop back on the bus and leave, my mother stamps over to the guide and says, You could've pointed to any of those manatees and said, *There's Karl*, and no one would've known the difference.

We want a new one, she tells him. Today. We aren't going anywhere until that happens.

The guide leaves and returns a half hour later with a picture of their new manatee, Tammy. Point her out to us, my mother says.

He indicates where she's floating and tells them how special she is, because she's already given birth twice.

For years, everything my mother does embarrasses me. The way she calls my name in crowded stores or roots in her enormous pocketbook like a raccoon through trash. She wears homemade clothes and scuffed brown pumps and never gets her hair wet. She forgets her checkbook when we eat out at a Chinese restaurant and makes me sit there as collateral while she goes back for it.

Some days, though, she's formidable. I'll never forget her coming home and telling me about staring down that guide before they left and saying, Nothing bad better happen to our new manatee. And how nothing did.

She and Ed date for almost a year. If she sees anyone after Ed, she never introduces me to him. I'm still in love with your father, she'll say, ten, twenty, thirty years after he died. I never doubt it. Why would I? She and I both know that nothing, no newborn baby, no dreamboat or beagle puppy, is easier to love than the dead.

Remember ant farms? my mother asks me on the telephone today. Remember scratch-and-sniff stickers? she says. She and I know how good it feels to think about things you haven't thought about in a while. Harmless, nearly forgotten things. Some of the stickers smelled like what they were supposed to smell like and some didn't, and every time you scratched them the smell grew fainter. Remember that? You had to make sure to ration it out because the stickers wouldn't last long. It was an object lesson. Remember? Scratching and knowing that every time you scratched, you were erasing the very thing you were savoring.

Three Augusts since my father died. Brittle flowers, red wind. I rise out of bed and open a window to let my room breathe, let some bitter starlit air inside, and a pair of birds fly into my room, one right after the other, so close I can hear the feather-on-bone flap of their wings. I search the house and wake my mother and we open all the windows and search together but we never do find them.

2.

CITY OF TREES

My wife and son and I move to California, to the edge of the desert. We rent an apartment for a few months until we find a house for sale on a dead-end street across from a park full of jacarandas and fan palms. Three bedrooms, lots of light, succulents and fruit trees in the front yard, a pool in the backyard. The list price is oddly affordable, lower than any other house in the neighborhood. In the disclosure paperwork, we find out that the previous owner, a woman named Marjory, died on the premises a few weeks before the house went on the market. In California you're required to disclose this but not how they died or exactly where they died, only that they died *on the premises*, so it could've been in the driveway, front yard, crawl space, bathtub. Our offer is one of many and the realtor suggests we write a letter to convince her family to sell to us. My wife begins by writing a candid, friendly note with a few embellishments, like how our son is going to love the pool even though he's still afraid of the water. For my part, I turn it into a groveling fabrication. I say it was love at first sight. I say we've walked our dog past the house dozens of times and fantasized about living in this very house, this blue stucco bungalow. I say we used to see Marjory in the front yard, and we'd wave to each other as we walked past her house, fantasizing. I say I knew the second I laid eyes on the house that we'd end up living there.

We did walk our dog by the house once. I saw an older woman in the yard and waved to her and she smiled but didn't wave back. I noticed something chalked on the sidewalk out front: *We are all in this to get her.* I stared at it, wondering who *her* referred to, and what getting her might entail, feeling bewildered dread until the message cohered and the last three words became one. We are all in this together.

Our offer is accepted. We paint the walls before we move in, pull up the carpet, replace it with bamboo-inspired laminate. We know she died on the premises: Everything else reveals itself in increments. Rogue menthol butts in the garden shed. Surprise spring poppies behind the garage. Spackle marks on the walls where her pictures once hung. We make sure to hang ours a bit lower, or higher.

* * *

After a shower, as I'm waiting for the bathroom mirror to unfog, I notice the faint outline of a butterfly in the bottom corner, a ghost decal from the previous owner. Butterflies were her favorite animal. Daily the house yields messages she sent to a future she would not see, and daily we do our best to etch them out. We retile her backsplash, remove her satellite dish, throw away her mail. We don't mean to starve her flowering olive trees but we do. We starve them. In the backyard sits an enormous metal sculpture of a butterfly. I promised Marjory's family we'd take good care of it, but it just sits there rusting and gathering bird shit and spiderwebs. The only time it gives me joy is when a living butterfly alights atop it. A solution teasing at the edge of a problem, mocking it. Sometimes my wife or I will spray it down with a hose, but when it dries it looks exactly the same.

    I walk Otis, our dog, along the flagstone path in our yard. The woman had the path installed, along with a lime tree, fig tree, persimmons, dwarf mandarins, and a tidy row of flowering olives, all of them now dying, or dead. Trees are extremely sympathetic, the landscaper told me when I asked what was wrong with them. At first I thought he meant that the trees were blighted from grief over the woman's death. He meant trees sympathize with other trees. Everyone seems to know this now but I didn't then. I had no idea that older trees nurture younger ones underground, or that when a beech tree is felled the forest will often sustain the stump, keeping it alive for decades.

* * *

His powder-blue cardigan hangs in the closet as it has in the twenty-two houses, apartments, and dorm rooms I've lived in since he died. I try it on about once a year, consider wearing it, but never do. It's too tight. I have a picture of him in the sweater and it fits him perfectly, even though he was bigger than me. Maybe it's shrunk. Twenty-two places, though I may be forgetting one or two. And it didn't always hang in the closet—some didn't have closets. My mother mails me the yellowed slip of paper with his name on it, the one she kept under her mattress after their first date. She says she's consolidating. No room in the condo for a slip of paper. My pile grows and grows while hers dwindles.

Three days a week I drive deeper into the desert to teach writing. This year the college unveiled a new slogan: *Come Here, Go Anywhere*. As if it's a regional airport, or a staging area for an exodus. The campus buildings look like medical offices fronted by vast shimmering parking lots, and I cruise row after row searching for an open space. I notice a student walking to his car. I lower my window and ask if he's leaving—he is, so I creep behind him until he locates his car. I walk through the lot, waving off any cars that slow down behind me, already in a foul mood.

In my office I find two fat robins perched on my desk. I left the window cracked over winter break and they must've squeezed inside. I open it wider and scare them out with a file folder, cursing the woman in the office next to mine who dumps birdseed on her windowsill to lure birds, who keeps a bowl of candy on her desk to lure students. Taped to her door is the saddest headline I've ever read: *Woman Offers $10,000 for Missing Cat*. The woman is her, the cat is Milton. I don't know if Milton has returned—the huge reward and the fact that the clipping is two years old suggest he has not.

Scrubbing acrid droppings from the floor, I notice on the bookshelf, neatly built atop a stack of unreturned student work, a small nest. Twigs, feathers, bits of grass, a straw wrapper. Inside the nest are three blue eggs. I stare at them, unable to reckon what I'm seeing with the painted cinder-block walls and tube lighting of my office. Finally, I find some student newspapers, cover my desk and floor with them, and open the window as wide as it will go in hopes the birds will return. I gather whatever books I might need during the next few weeks and leave.

A man knocks on our front door. He wants to sell me a phony alarm-company sign to plant in our front yard. Don't you want to protect your family? he asks. All your neighbors have one. Except you.

Real ones or fake ones? I ask. He nods and says, Exactly.

My wife paints the front door canary yellow. I spend four days clumsily uprooting the flowering olive trees and planting bougainvillea and night-blooming jasmine. We eat dinner out back, Otis waiting patiently for our son to drop food, the sun setting in a sky of pink shivering fire.

The kids in the house behind ours stand on the roof of their playhouse and peek over the fence while we eat. There are three of them, twin boys and a girl. They don't make any noise so whenever my wife or I spot them we always wonder how long they've been there. It's unnerving. They have white-blond hair and the serene, already-gone look of cult children.

What's his name again? a twin asks.

Dog, man, or boy? my wife says.

Boy, he says.

My son tells them. Can we come over and swim sometime? they ask. My son says yes and they hop the fence, take off their shirts, jump into the pool.

Soon we hear the sound of a bell ringing in the house behind ours and the kids hop out of the pool and climb back over the fence, dripping wet. The next day my wife finds a note on our front door: *Sorry about that yesterday. It won't happen again. They've been told 1,000 times how important it is to respect the property line.*

I remember kids in school whose parents wrote their last name on everything they owned: lunch box, calculator, baseball hat, backpack. Nothing of mine ever felt like it belonged to me. When Thriller came out my mother made me a Michael Jackson glove. She hemmed an old evening glove and hand-stitched hundreds of sequins onto it, and I brought it to school. Everyone wanted a turn with it, and by the end of the day it was gone. I was sad and relieved. Let someone else be its caretaker, I thought. Now I walk the perimeter of my property every morning committing what's mine to memory. That shed's mine, this tree's mine, that one beyond the fence is my neighbor's, which drops poison berries into my yard, which is mine. Now I know why we build fences, not for protection but for separation. To remind us where our claims no longer obtain.

Right before our son goes to the bathroom he calls out, Can snakes get into houses? He's afraid of a snake hiding in the plumbing. I don't know whether it's something he heard about at school or an innate fear, a remnant from back when we used to crouch in the savanna to relieve ourselves.

No, my wife calls back, snakes cannot get into houses.

He, too, is learning the importance of the property line. When ants infest our kitchen, he and I use chalk to draw a perimeter around the outside of the house like detectives at the scene of a murder. Can't the ants just walk across the line? he says. It's special chalk, I tell him, specially designed to repel them. That night he comes into our room and says he's afraid. You're fine, I call out from the edge of sleep. Special chalk, I say. But he's not worried about ants anymore. He worries about the next thing and, after that, the next.

* * *

He and I watch fan-made Peter Pan cartoon compilation videos set to the eighties rock ballads of my childhood. After three or four of them I'm often on the verge of tears. One day he asks me what Captain Hook's name was before he lost his hand. I check into Hook's details and read out his birth name to my son: James Aloysius Hook. His name was Hook before the hook—having his hand cut off and fed to a crocodile was a terrible irony. Or a terrible coincidence.

Back in college, I tell him, I had a friend, George Blaze. Guess how he died?

My son covers his ears. He doesn't want to know how George Blaze died. Later he asks if there's such a thing as a monster planet. I ask him to clarify what he means and he says, A planet with only monsters on it. How am I supposed to answer a question like this? I answer yes. Which makes him happy (I knew it would) and a little apprehensive. How close is it?

I pause for some quick calculations. At least ninety-seven light-years away, I tell him. Which is very far, I say. A light-year's like a normal year but much longer because it's a distance. You know how long a year feels, January to December? Okay, so imagine that but you're walking the entire time, through space. For ninety-seven years. That's how far.

He asks why it's called a light-year and I say, No one's really sure, and put my hand on his shoulder, consoling him about all the things we want to know and cannot.

* * *

The city council voted to ban the ice-cream man from our town. From our house on its western edge we can hear his music slowly approach and recede, approach and recede, as if testing the durability of our town limits. My son sits in our front yard holding a dollar bill, waiting for the truck to turn onto our street.

A friend of mine is taking his son ice fishing in northern Minnesota, just like he did with his father when he was a kid. Sitting in an ice shanty with a freezing pole, he says, was a yearly tradition. It's one of his earliest memories. He shows me his ice auger, his ice axe. They use sonar now, so instead of fishing one hole they walk around drilling hundreds of holes. He invites me and my son to go with them, but I can't imagine buying boots and parkas and plane tickets to tag along. I wish I'd inherited some tradition from my father, even if it meant going to northern Minnesota. I wonder what manly things we might've done together had he lived. Probably something with horses. Riding them, shoeing them, teaching them our names. With my own son, I'm mostly trying to be present, to be open and known. We can invent our own traditions along the way. One year for Christmas, after we decorated the tree, I hoisted him up to put the star atop it. That's our tradition now. We do it every year, and we'll continue to, even after he gets too big to hoist. Anything can be a tradition if you repeat it a few times.

* * *

Our town moved Halloween to a Monday this year. I didn't know they could do that. We start decorating the house in September, and well before Halloween hot winds blow our novelty tombstones into neighbors' yards. I'm tired of retrieving them. Let the graves of the novelty dead go unmarked, I say.

Real spiders move into the fake spider webs, crows circle endlessly...

Our son makes his own costume. It's a tradition. He came up with it in July and never wavered. His friends are going as ninjas, pirates, superheroes—our son is going as the food pyramid. His costume is a nutritional diagram. It's what happens when you tell him he can be whatever he wants. He takes it as a challenge. He made it out of cardboard, grains at the base, fats and oils at the top. It's as big as he is. I cut an old belt and threaded it through the back so he can carry the pyramid around like a signboard.

My wife stays home to dole out candy. Because our house is on a dead-end street, our trick-or-treaters consist mostly of teens taking a break from getting stoned in the park. They don't bother with costumes. At the door my wife asks them what they're dressed as before she gives them candy. A sleepwalker, they say. Indolence, they say. Nature's ache. A winnowing replica of myself.

No, no. This is what we wish they'd say. What they really say is: Um. And: I can't remember. And: I'm dressed as him and he's dressed as me. They return again and again forgetting, or thinking she forgot, they were there.

I fill a thermos with cold red wine and follow him and his friends from house to house. I wait on the sidewalk while they run to the front door of a ranch house. Next to me stands a mom in a Tinker Bell costume, low-cut top and shimmery leggings. How cute, she says as my son's friend approaches. How precious, she says to the other friend. How… informative, she says to my son.

I ask her if she always dresses up for Halloween. When else would we dress up? she answers, shuffling her daughter away. The daughter's a different, more orthodox Tinker Bell.

Our neighbors pass out candy stingily, one piece per child. A woman leaning down to hold the collar of a pug in a bumblebee suit asks my son if he's trying to make a statement with his costume, and he tells her he just wanted to be something no one else was.

So, in other words, yes, she says.

I don't hear this exchange. My son tells me about it when we're far enough away that he knows I can't do anything about it. He doesn't want me coming to his rescue. He knows adults are random, erratic, mostly harmless.

I carry his pyramid home. I tell him he can eat as much candy as he wants until we get there. We come upon a darkened house with some people out front. On the lawn an elderly man is slumped in a swinging chair with a horrible look on his face. Surprise mixed with sorrow. In his lap is a silver bowl, and the people are discussing whether the man's dead or just posed as a spooky decoration. A woman says she knows him and this is the sort of thing he does on Halloween. That's why the bowl's there. As soon as one of us reaches in, he's going to scare us.

I recognize the house but not him. His chest isn't moving and his hand grips the chain in an unnatural way. He's dead, I'm sure of it. Someone should check on him, I say. Everyone seems content to just stand there. I move closer. The bowl in his lap is filled with fun-size Milky Ways, and I reach out to move it.

Thief! he shouts, lurching forward.

Everyone laughs. Apparently they're in on it too. They've been standing there for hours, doing the same thing to everyone who passes. Tricking them by telling them exactly what's going to happen. What a night, when you can be resuscitated by a stranger. When you can be something no one else was.

Join us, they say. Help us find our next victim.

The limits of my language, Wittgenstein says, are the limits of my town. Something to that effect. We are bisected by freeways, circled by helicopters, tilted up toward the foothills, snug in our stalls. Our town is a blend of street noise and birdsong, a flurry of signs, an algebra problem. People call it a bedroom community, a phrase I repeat because it sounds kind of lurid until I finally look up what bedroom community means.

They also call it the City of Trees because of the trees. Along Foothill, sycamores with their tops sheared to accommodate power lines. On Harrison, massive peeling eucalyptuses. On Cambridge, prim maidenhairs dropping their rancid fruit. Our town is a page, its streets are the lines, houses are words, and the people: punctuation. Trees are just trees. I hear church bells on Sunday but never see anyone coming out or going in. A new sign next to the Church of Christ says HE'S STILL LISTENING and it makes me a little sad. It makes me want to say something worth listening to.

I read somewhere that memories are temporary constellations, projected by the mind only for as long as they're needed. Years from now when my son looks back, what I'd like is for him to remember me as a vital but inconspicuous presence, rushing ahead to open doors and stepping aside.

When we visit Florida he and I go to the racetrack my father managed. I haven't been in thirty years. On the way, I tell him about the old gamblers sizing up the horses before races, about his coworkers who spoke to me as if they already knew me. All the mystery and promise of the adult world resided here when I was his age. The track is seedy now, depressing. Maybe it always was. A bar full of day drunks waiting for an OTB race to start, pledging allegiance as the national anthem plays on TV. I thought maybe I'd write an essay or something about fathers and horses and sons. I ask around but no one remembers my father—I waited too long. And horses no longer race here, just greyhounds. I buy popcorn and we walk through the concourse and into the stands to get a better view of the track. I've told him a few things about my father. He played basketball in college. He worked with horses. My son knows that he died young but it doesn't alarm him. Why should it? We stand at the rail, watching groundskeepers tend to the track. I remember my mother telling me a story about the money room, about how my father got locked inside. As a kid, I pictured a room made of money. I ask the bartender where the money room is and he looks at me like I'm crazy.

You mean the ATM? he says.

Back at my mother's condo my son asks her what I was like at his age. She says, He was a good eater.

He wants to know more. Did I help around the house? Did I cry when I found out my dad died? I don't think so, she tells him. But he cried a lot as a baby. He had a mirror in his crib and he'd stare at it and cry and cry.

Why'd you leave a mirror in the crib if it made him cry? he asks.

She thinks about it for a second and says, To keep him busy.

* * *

She knows Halloween is his favorite holiday so she buys him a stack of spooky books. Not scary, spooky—a fine distinction that grandmother and grandson intuitively grasp. She sits with him on the couch as he reads about friendly witches and vegan vampires. They go to a movie together and he returns with a ukelele. They watch how-to videos on her computer. She helps him tune it and plink out chords. Where was this version of her when I was a kid? The teacher, the patient companion. I know the answer: It didn't exist yet. But I wish I saw some trace of it. As we're flying back to California he finds a ten-dollar bill in the pocket of his jeans. A speech bubble next to Hamilton telling him his Grandmére loves him.

On my morning run I like to imagine myself at age ten watching me pass. There he goes again, I think of me thinking. Back when I was young and strong I felt weak. Now that I'm old and weak I feel strong. You should see my toolbox. I've got a socket set that could dismantle a space station. A hammer for any possible occasion. Casual hammers, vulgar hammers, somber, pragmatic hammers. Tooth chisel, stork-beak pliers, sandpaper with the coarsest allowable grit. Decades I've spent accruing tools for any contingency, remembering all the ground I conceded when I was younger. The kid who stole my BMX bike and spray-painted it gold. The girl who called me a grub. The teacher correcting me for saying *predicament*, insisting it was pronounced *prediclament*. Every exchange ends in a scrum, one side shoving, the other being shoved. At night I lie in bed scoring the day, ground gained and ground lost, enemies neutralized, until white noise stuns me to sleep.

Sometimes I dream of tunneling to a more accommodating age. Early 1800s, Great Plains. My possessions come in bunches: fetish beads, pelts, quiver of poison-tipped arrows, four horses minimum. One for raids, one for riding, one for companionship, and another for companionship. I'd be too buried in my existence to be puzzled by it. I wouldn't freeze-dry my days by writing things down. I wouldn't need to *speak*. My only repartee would be the silent arc of a poison arrow. Got any plans for the long weekend? Poison arrow. Paper or plastic? Poison arrow. Can you initial here, here, and here? Poison arrow, poison arrow, poison arrow.

I die where I fall, young and without delay. I'm cleaned by scavenger birds. To my son I bequeath an acute sense of scale. And pelts. He'll know me by my horses, now his. My last words... I won't have any last words.

I hardly ever dream about my father anymore. Often I wake up feeling strongly about something but by the time my head clears I can't remember what it is.

* * *

I spent my twenties and thirties bristling against rules, limitations, boundaries. I skid into my forties well aware of certain certainties. I'll never visit the blue hills of Estonia or the Tower of Silence in Yazd. I'll never pilot or captain a goddamn thing. My talents, such as they are, are nontransferable. Jigsaw puzzles, partial recall, small talk with strangers. Here is the key to small talk: let most of what strangers say pass right through you untasted, like medicine.

You look awfully familiar, I tell the cashier at the hardware store.

So I've been told, she says.

We talk, we make our triangulations, but still I can't figure out how I know her. I leave with my bagful of parts, clicking the alarm fob to find my car in the parking lot.

Later I realize how I know the woman from the hardware store. I know her from the hardware store.

Another sign, in front of the Methodist church: GOD ISN'T ANGRY. Whenever I pass it, I say it aloud, God isn't angry, adding the unspoken verdict: He's just… disappointed.

The bombs never came like I thought they would. The Cold War ends. The dread subsides. My mother quits smoking. She drinks less. She wins teacher of the year, is diagnosed with cervical cancer, survives, breast cancer, survives. She never dates again. I quit fretting over my own extinction. I let my childhood scab and scar. I enroll at community college, then transfer to the state college. I impound my aspirations, look for myself in other people, major in anthropology, the study of people, go from one air-conditioned building to another. I sell my plasma for twenty-four dollars. I smoke hash. I want to be like the stellar burnouts at the Silver Q, but drugs make me feel dull and defective. I decide to become an architect. I sit around drinking and talking about negative space with classmates. I wear nonprescription glasses. I develop a talent for vociferousness. In a poetry class I write a sestina about the last time I saw my father. A girlfriend copies it onto cardstock and frames it and gives it to my mother, who hangs it in the guest bathroom, eye level when you're taking a dump. My design professor convinces me I'm a better wannabe writer than wannabe architect without reading a word I've written. I change majors. I write a story based on the sestina about the last time I saw my father. My writing professor scribbles *poorly resuscitated autobiography* on it. Fiction, he says, concerns itself not with what *did* happen but with what *should* happen. In class he plays Jimi Hendrix's version of All Along the Watchtower. Write like that, he tells us. I quit writing about my father. I fall in love with a poet and move to Arizona. We get married. We buy towels, silverware, a bread machine. We have a son. I cook dinner with him in a sling on my back. I watch him sleep. I start running. I want to be around to see as much of his life as I can. I think about my own father again and a new sentiment creeps in. Not sadness. Not dread or nostalgia. Something like fear. Imagining myself in that hospital room, my son at my bedside, and maybe he'll remember it and maybe he won't. Maybe I want him to and maybe I don't. We move to Washington, Ohio, Iowa, Pennsylvania, Vermont. We find a beagle lost on the state highway and bring him home. I wear prescription glasses. We move to California.

My mother calls on my father's birthday. We play a round of I remember. I remember him in his faux-leather recliner laughing at the nightly news and my resentment because I couldn't figure out what was funny. She remembers the time she wanted Freddy Fender's autograph. Do I? He was performing at the horse track and she couldn't go. My father didn't want to ask, but eventually he gave in and brought an autographed picture home for her: *You're the tear in my eye. Freddy Fender.* After he died, she looked at it closely and realized it was my father's handwriting.

Yes, I say. I remember. By which I mean: I remember being told about it. I like hearing the story again though. I like the ones where he cuts a plausible figure. Not a doomed father or favored son but a man who did things simply to amuse himself.

Laughter's meant to be shared, she says. She watched a documentary about it. It's a universal language, she says. Even before humans could talk, we laughed. I can't remember why. Something to do with surviving danger, the overwhelming relief of it.

What else? she says to fill the silence (on his birthday, it's hard to get her off the phone), and she waits and I wait to see which one of us knows the answer.

She googles the distance between her condo and our new house, to remind herself. Twenty-five hundred and eleven miles. She can't get over it. If you could somehow drive door-to-door without stopping for gas it would take thirty-five hours. Thirty-five hours from her only son. A friend of hers calls it a *hostile distance*, the kind of distance you put between yourself and something you want nothing to do with. And my mother doesn't agree or disagree, but it's too far.

Airplanes, I say. Leave in the morning and get here before dinner.

I thought you liked Florida, she says.

I do, I say.

Now that you've escaped it, she says, sighing. You always wanted to be somewhere you weren't. Remember the magic store?

Yes, Mom. I remember everything. Wanting to be in school while at home, home while in school, *in* the movie while at the movies.

She doesn't believe me when I tell her the only college that offered me a job was here on the edge of the desert. She names every college in Florida that she can think of, tells me she knows someone who knows someone who works in the computer lab who can put in a word.

Finally she says, I always thought we were close. I mean spiritually. No, I don't mean spiritually, but more like...

On the first day of class she asks her students to draw where they live. She says some kids can't even picture what their house looks like from the outside. These are the happy ones.

The kids write her thank-you cards when the school year ends. She loves them. Not the kids but the cards. She stickpins them like exotic butterflies to the corkboard in the utility closet she uses as an office. She mails my son fifty dollars and a stationery set for his birthday, each card monogrammed with his initials in florid cursive, just so he can crack open the box and send her one.

How often do you think about your mother? What's the recommended daily allowance? One time? Three? We never offered each other much consolation or came to a tolerable understanding. I know that. I couldn't wait to leave for college. Even so, I was homesick for months. Ten times a day? For my thirty-ninth birthday she mails me a T-shirt: FUTURE BEST-SELLING AUTHOR. I could laugh it off, could write her a thank-you card, but it infuriates me. I throw it away in its packaging while my son looks on, push it to the very bottom of the trash. Twice an hour? Not thoughts—memories, feelings, involuntary spasms of resentment and guilt. I used to tell people she cried when I dropped out of architecture school but in reality she didn't care. She never burdened me with expectations or unsolicited advice. Before I published a word, a high school friend was already performing liver transplants. My mother never doubted the wisdom of what I was doing or questioned how long it was taking. She let me create my own doubts and rationalizations. Now she drives to libraries and bookstores, tells the counterperson to order copies of her son's book. And often they do. Put me in your next one, she says to me. Change my name and make me smarter. She's never read a thing I've written. Actually, that's not true: I mailed her one of the stories I wrote in college, a rip-off of The Swimmer called The Mower where a man clips his way home on a riding lawn mower. She wrote back: *I am so proud of you!! The story seems really deep. It's deep, right?*

I abandon my campus office to the nesting robins. I hold office hours in the student center, an atrium attached to a food court: Pizza Hut, Taco Bell, Denny's. A student comes by to discuss a Chekhov story. She doesn't get it, she says. I walk her through it, pointing out how a repeated detail accumulates meaning, and she sighs. Why does everything have to *mean* something? she says. Can't something just *be* something?

I tell her about the woman who lived in the house we bought. She planted a tomato garden in the backyard before she died.

The tomatoes came in without help and we started eating them. They were delicious, I say, maybe the best I've ever tasted. Little pear tomatoes we ate right off the vine. But it's complicated by the fact that the woman who planted them is dead now. She's an inextricable part of their taste.

The student nods like she understands what I'm talking about. Then, very tentatively, she says: So the woman who lived in your house... she's buried in that garden?

Make awful things happen to your characters, I tell them, quoting Vonnegut. How else will you know what they're made of? My students oblige. They kill and maim their characters, drag them behind cars, experiment on them, marry them to serial killers, lock them in airless basements, get them hooked on flesh-eating drugs, chain them to boulders, cook them into meat for dragons. Their life expectancy is about ten pages. Things will be going smoothly—a protagonist out for a scenic drive—and in the final sentence she'll wrench the wheel and sail off a cliff.

What are their characters made of? Bones, blood, brittle tissue.

Go easy on your characters, I say now. It's not their fault they were born into your story. Give them friends, a reliable car, health insurance, a nice pair of ankle boots. How about a surprise party? A serene inner life, parents who don't outlive them. Have you ever found money in an old pair of pants? Write about that maybe. Reach into your pocket and feel those folded, slightly powdery bills, knowing right away what they are, and hesitate, revel in that hesitation, before you pull them out and see what you have.

I am supposed to be painting our mailbox but I'm distracted by men doing karate in the park. They spar on flattened cardboard, punching, blocking, driving their opponents to the ground. I remember how in school pretend fights led to real fights, but the men help each other up and then they all link arms, huddle like a team after a game. They are praying. Barefoot, they pray for a long time. Some wave when they notice me, and I respond with a gesture created just for them, a neat two-finger salute followed by a nod. The gesture says: Morning, gentlemen. It says: I admire your fighting style. But: I feel an urge to call the police on you. Not out of malice, no, but because the idea of a uniformed officer busting up your circle comforts me. I mean, here you are out in the park on this beautiful Sunday afternoon ritualizing your animosity toward one another. Extracting it like venom, combining it, turning it into antivenom. Why can't I figure out how to do this when I play poker with other fathers in the neighborhood? Instead I drink too much, talk too much, lose eighty dollars, and wake up to a text from another father that says, *Goddamn, your impersonation of the dead sailor last night was hilarious*, which I'm happy to hear except I have no recollection of impersonating the dead sailor. I don't know how men make friends with other men. There seems to be a great deal of restraint involved. Probing sarcasm, buried circuitry. The gesture says: I used to know some karate too.

My son watches me paint from his bedroom window. I sweep the brush across the mailbox with overdramatic flourishes like a painting maestro, spattering the sidewalk. I pantomime an excited discussion with him, mouthing words without making a sound. He does the same, gesturing wildly to stress his point. Back and forth we go, our karaoke becoming more animated, until he gets bored and waves goodbye to me.

I tell him stories about Sensei Duane, embellishing a few details. I say he was trying to assemble an army of boys without fathers for reasons he never made clear. I say he had a pet capuchin monkey. I say he taught us a hundred different submission holds to disable attackers. I pinch the flesh where his neck meets his shoulder and tell him, This is the Shah, the hundredth most powerful submission hold. I pinch the meaty part of his hand. This is the Smurf Bite, number ninety-eight. The Stunner, ninety-four. The Crab Claw, ninety-three. I promise to teach him one per year. He does the math in his head. Can you start with the most powerful one? he asks me.

* * *

My father had five years left when he was my age now. I don't know what to do with this awareness, except write a song about it: *Five years left when he was my age now.* That's it so far. A friend who's gone back to school to become a family therapist says it's common to be aware of milestones like this. Or he says it's not uncommon, which is the more therapeutic phrase. He says it's perfectly healthy, or perfectly not unhealthy. Five years until I reach my father's age when he died, and one year until my son reaches mine. I like to think I'll start to mellow when those milestones arrive because I'll have lived long enough, and my son will be old enough, to dispel whatever mystique mothers and fathers acquire when they die young. We can enter a new demystified age and he'll know me and I'll know him and all will be well.

The former German ambassador to Japan is staying in the house next door while he teaches a visiting seminar at a local college. He is a friendly man, full of questions. Daily my son accidentally kicks his soccer ball over the fence, into his backyard, and by the next morning the ball has been tossed back into our yard.

He asks my son who he's rooting for in the World Cup and my son says Germany. The ambassador smiles. My son hates Germany. The team, I mean. He likes France, the team, because they always win, and Greece because his grandfather is Greek. Later, I ask why he told the ambassador he's rooting for Germany and my son says, Because he's German.

* * *

He's constantly tuning and retuning himself to his environment, sensing conditions and responding to them. He didn't learn this from me. It's like how people living near the desert start to resemble the desert, and people in the far north start to resemble ice. Maybe that's why I'm here, to notice this attunement, to record it.

I listen as my wife and son reach a compromise on how long he's allowed to watch highlights of people playing video games. The sheer number of words it takes to raise a child—it's absurd. We talk him out of bed and to school in the morning, through dinner and back into bed. We talk him through dentist appointments and swim lessons and haircuts. At the airport I pull up a live map on my laptop that shows all the planes in the air, hundreds of airplane shapes tethered by electronic lines to their points of departure. Look, I say to him, look how common it is, what we're about to do.

Escorting him through childhood on a flotilla of words. I remember the wannabe Amish guy who tended the video store cash register with his daughter next to him in a playpen, twenty years ago. One night I came in and he was showing her trading cards with pictures of medieval court dwarfs on them. Silently he'd hand her a card and silently she'd study it and hand it back to him. When he noticed me he said, I want to teach her that the world isn't as uncomplicated as she thinks it is.

A worthy enough goal, I guess. My son says he watched footage of ocean trenches at the neighbors' house, and there are these blind white eels that break apart if you bring them to the surface—they're held together by water pressure—and they terrified him. I tell him not to worry because he'll never have to go to the bottom of the ocean. You're better off worrying about the DMV, I say.

He walks off without asking what DMV stands for. He doesn't need to. His sense of danger is prehistoric, wiser than words.

What scared me most as a kid? Broken teeth, silence behind doors, dead father watching over while I masturbated, shaking his head. Dead father shaking his head when I missed a layup, when I failed my middle school placement tests on purpose. Back then it seemed obvious that the living could do nothing but disappoint the dead.

I used to call the local library for a bedtime story, I tell my son, recalling it fondly. Fatherless kid, mother off at the community college, dialing up a librarian to tell him a story about a magic pebble. My son looks at me like it's the saddest thing he's ever heard.

It wasn't actually my bedtime, I say.

Even sadder, his look says.

* * *

He listens to an old song that goes, *I am, I am, I am Superman, and I can do anything,* and he asks me whether the singer is saying *can* or *can't.*

Can, I say.

The chorus repeats and he asks me again and I reassure him again. He has no tolerance for brooding superheroes who can't do certain things. He likes Superman. He suspects he's only pretending to be afraid of kryptonite, the way he pretends to be Clark Kent. The characters in his cartoon shows never use words like *kill* or *die.*

We must eliminate them! says the skeleton lord.

Punish them, destroy them, terminate them, vanquish them.

Temporarily, of course. No one dies. Even the blackest-hearted villains survive into the next episode, and the next. When the skeleton lord's air fleet is brought down, the sky blooms with the black parachutes of healthy skeletons. My son leans closer to the television, willing each of them safely back to their evil lair.

Otis has a tumor on his spine. We take him to the vet to be put to sleep when our son comes home from school. He's inconsolable. He thinks it's his fault. I was too rough, he says. I sat on him and he yelped. We assure him it wasn't his fault. Will they bury him? he asks. No, my wife says, and we wait for the next question but he doesn't ask. We try to comfort him by remembering funny things about Otis. How he thought his barking was what made the mailman go away. The time he jumped up and stole a pizza slice out of my wife's hand. I write a remembrance with a picture of Otis sitting next to our son as a newborn and hang it on the refrigerator. He's sad the next morning but by the time he returns home from school he's pretty well over it. We stow Otis's leash and collar and bowls and bed and chew toys in the garage along with the box of cremains. We display his picture on a bookshelf. It's okay to be sad, I tell our son. He knows. Otis was a good boy, I say. Good right until the end. Remember the tip of white on his tail? Remember him waiting patiently at your high chair for you to throw him cereal? Stoking the embers. I don't know why I want him to grieve a little longer.

A few months later a long-haired calico shows up in our backyard and we let her inside. He names her Wendy.

He doesn't remember the bats in the first house he lived in. One morning we discovered a pair of them perched in the curtains above his bed. The doctor didn't find any bite marks but recommended rabies shots just in case. He doesn't recall the shots or the bats or how I cooked with him in a sling. Or the neighbor who knew he loved fire engines and arranged for the station to park a hook-and-ladder truck on our street. He has one memory of our years across from the battlefield: me dropping him on the ice. He describes my orange coat, the ugly Iowa beanie I used to wear, and tumbling out of my arms. That winter, freezing rain made rock-hard berms of ice all over town. I had to free our car with an ax to go to the library. As I pulled him out of his car seat I slipped and fell on my side, shielding him from the brunt of the impact. He was fine. I bruised a rib and had to sleep upright in a chair long after the ice melted. I couldn't sneeze or laugh. He remembers none of this. It was scary, he says. You dropped me on the ice.

The ice melted to reveal two dead squirrels in the park—he asked what happened and I told him they fell asleep when it started to snow, which terrified him. For years he connected falling asleep with dying. He doesn't remember that either. Shuddering awake and turning on his light, even in the dead of summer, to make sure it wasn't snowing in his bedroom.

At IKEA he asks why there are so many pregnant women shopping and I tell him I'm not sure. He asks if women go to IKEA to get pregnant, and although I'm intrigued by the idea, I restrain myself from telling him that, yes, they do. I say maybe they do. He asks if I knew that French women are naked 30 percent of the time, and I tell him I did not. Where did he hear this? He says it's just something he knows. He says he knows a lot of things his mother and I don't. It seems like lately he's trying to keep himself a mystery. When we tell him he needs to go brush his teeth, he says, I did it yesterday. When we insist, he says, Does a tiger brush his teeth?

The only story he wants to hear is Dracula and Frankenstein Are Friends. My mother bought it for him. I've read it hundreds of times. I've memorized it, I dream about it. I no longer say, Who will bob for all these apples? in Frankenstein's voice, or, This party's lost its spice, in Dracula's voice. I read fast and without joy, never missing a word, because if I do he'll insist I read it over.

Dracula and Frankenstein are friends. They live side-by-side in a town where the houses are all spooky.

I tell him there are thousands of stories better than this one. Literally every story ever told, for example. The girl who can't stop dancing. The flute player who rounds up children like rats. The chicken who crosses the road. He doesn't want those. He wants to hear about how Dracula and Frankenstein are friends.

I can't do it anymore. I tell him the book has to go away for a while. Stories are like people, I say. They get tired. How about tonight I make a story up for you?

About people dying? he asks. Somehow he got it into his head that I write only about people dying. I say he can choose. And if he doesn't like where it's going he can say stop. He thinks about it.

A scary one, he says. But not too scary.

Happy monsters, that's what he likes. He doesn't care how they became monsters, or whether they're waiting for a maiden's kiss to turn them human again.

I begin: Once upon a time there was a boy lost in the woods. Stop, he says.

I tell my students about Chekhov's ashtray and Hemingway's sausage grinder and Nabokov's fondled detail. I tell them about Kafka, lungs full of tuberculosis and unable to speak, writing fragments on slips of paper and handing them to friends: *Yesterday evening a late bee drank the white lilac dry*. And: *How wonderful that is, isn't it? The lilac—dying, it drinks, goes on swilling.* So sad! they say. Notice what you notice, I tell them. Look closely at things. We'll try! they say. On my drive home I struggle to remember the last time I looked closely at things.

A mitten thumbtacked to the gnarled magnolia by the senior center. Disembodied cocks spray-painted on the middle school portables. The moment right before a pair of city buses cross paths on Foothill when it's unclear whether or not the bus drivers will wave to each other. One afternoon some other parents and I are at the elementary school waiting for the bell to ring. A father does some shirtless pull-ups on the jungle gym. Then he walks over to the flagpole and grips it with both arms and thrusts his body sideways, legs extended. His abdomen is as stiff as an insect's glossy exoskeleton. We are trapped, unable to move, bearing witness to something private, slightly obscene. When he hops down I'm so relieved that I feel like clapping. I clap.

Overnight every tree in town has been painted at the trunk with either a red X or a blue O. My wife and I walk through the park, trying to discern a pattern. A few of the palms are marked with X's. All the jacarandas are marked with O's.

Tic-tac-toe, I say.

The lone sycamore: a bleeding blue O. They're sentences, she says. The trunks are subjects, branches are predicates, and roots are the underlying, the hidden...

Then I see a leafless elm with a red X and understand. They're death sentences. Someone's delivered judgment, decided which trees will be cut down and which will remain. I call parks and rec and a woman with a vaguely Slavic smear to her consonants confirms our suspicions. No second opinion? I ask, and she laughs a cackling laugh. I picture a mouth full of dull silver.

Days pass. The coyotes return. At night my wife and I lie in bed listening to their teasing calls. The death-row trees remain. Doomed bottlebrushes flower, doomed ginkgos sprout doomed berries. A friend who beat cancer has a rowan tree with fifty-one leaves tattooed to his chest. One for each year he's been alive. He plans to add a new leaf every spring. The friend (his name's Andrew—calling him *the friend* makes him sound imaginary) says that when he starts to feel despair or dread he's going to close his eyes and picture the tree on his chest thickening with leaves.

Sunday mornings, we walk our dogs together. Or used to. Now I walk dogless with him and his dog. Did you know people with one-syllable names are the happiest? he asks me. A new study just came out. Call me Drew from now on.

Whenever a car in a driveway is blocking part of the sidewalk, he kicks the bumper as we walk past.

Bad car, he tells his dog.

We invite a neighbor over for dinner. He says that it's the strangest thing: even though we've lived here over a year the house still smells like Marjory. He raises his chin and sniffs. He has tiny teeth, gray as shark skin. Maybe she smelled like the house, my wife says. I'm not sure what sort of distinction she's making but I feel better for it. On my third glass of wine I ask whether Marjory died inside the house or outside. He has no idea. One day an ambulance pulled up and took her. Morning? Afternoon? Night? Let's change the subject, he says, and looks around and asks me if the floors are real bamboo. Bamboo-inspired laminate, I tell him. He says, Wow. You'd have to be a floor guy to tell the difference.

Our house makes a buzzing sound. Nobody but me hears it. My son follows me around as I try to locate its source. We stop in the bathroom. In his bedroom. He says he thinks he hears it.

You do? I say. Maybe not, he says. We walk outside and listen. I hear birdsong and the clinking of men playing horseshoes in the park, but no buzzing. I hear the buzzing sound only when I'm not listening for it.

I hear it while my wife and I watch a zombie movie. I go into our bedroom, the kitchen, then into our son's room, where he's asleep clutching a sock monkey. I watch him and the sound starts up again but it's either very faint or very far. As soon as I leave his room it disappears. I return just as the zombies claim another victim. They rejoice in another kill and stumble on.

The quality that comes to mind when I think of the town house where my mother and I lived is silence. Even though the TV was always on and she was often talking on the phone, neither of us had the means to say what needed saying. One year on my birthday she served me a giant mound of bacon because I'd claimed I could eat as much as she put in front of me. I don't remember saying this but I did. I ate all of it. She watched. When I finished I felt close to vomiting. I didn't admit this, or thank her, but she knew. That pleased spark in her eye: finally I got exactly what I was asking for.

* * *

Next to her in her Pulsar, I used to signal to semitruck drivers on the highway, trying to get them to blow their air horns. I wanted influence, I wanted to be recognized by the biggest things on the road. I try this with my son in the car, and when the truck driver answers with a sustained honk, my son sinks low in his seat, mortified. He makes me promise to never do it again. I promise that I'll try. My son tells me I say *maybe* too much. He says that *we'll see* is not a satisfying answer. But shouldn't I be teaching him the subtle language of the road? He's ten years old, older than I was when I started to understand all the messages passed wordlessly from person to person to person.

I feel dimly accused when I see my name in someone else's handwriting. Junk mail now comes in hand-addressed envelopes. I open them and find coupons for bankruptcy lawyers and discount windows. What a relief it is. Something that demands no scrutiny from me. Something I can discard.

A package arrives in the mail, addressed to me. Inside are two demented-looking teddy bears and a note with the heading *In Memory of Eloise Sudduth and Freddie Vaughn.* My father's mother and sister. I haven't been in touch with them in years. After some internet searching and a few phone calls I find out that they both died earlier this year, my grandmother first, then my aunt three months later. My grandmother was ninety-one.

My aunt, sixty-four. Old age, complications from diabetes. They left everything, the family heirlooms, what was left of my father's belongings—his clothes and golf clubs, his picture on the nightstand—to their church and to a Baptist college in the middle of Kentucky to set up scholarships in his name. The house and everything inside it have been sold. All that was salvaged was a handful of their sleep shirts, which were cut up by someone from their church and filled with stuffing and made into demented-looking teddy bears.

To my surprise my son wants them in his room. He's always had a soft spot for misfit toys. I don't tell him who made them, or why. I don't know where to start. I try to muster something resembling a conclusive feeling about them. I keep coming back to how soon my aunt died after my grandmother. Like a brokenhearted lover, my mother says when we talk about it.

I can't remember why we stopped talking. Do I have to remember everything? Nobody, nothing, escaped their judgment, except themselves and my father. When my mother was figuring out how to pay for my braces, she asked them for help. No, they said. He'll just end up mouthing off and get his teeth knocked out. Maybe I'm leaving out something that would explain this, make sense of it. All I have are fragments. Like how at church with them the pastor asked us to pray for cities. Not ones destroyed by earthquakes or tsunamis, but San Francisco, land of fog and perdition. How hard we prayed for San Francisco. Or the glee in my grandmother's voice when she looked at a wall of old photographs and said: I just love traditions. Which ones? I asked, and she ignored me. Slavery? I said, and she snapped at me: Florida had slaves too! When I asked too many questions—about why they never listened to music, about the difference between their church and the Black Baptist church up the street, about my father and grandfather—they'd ask why I wanted to know. They'd say, You act like you're writing a book. They said it so much I started to believe it.

Every time I visited them in Kentucky I took something of his home with me. Silk handkerchief. Cut-glass ashtray with my last name on it. Basketball trophy, cheap watch, photographs. Slowly I would bleed them of my inheritance.

My mother reminds me: as a wedding gift, my grandmother gave them an old cuckoo clock, the only thing her ancestors brought with them when they came to America. A cuckoo clock and the clothes on their backs. I remember him waking before dawn to wind it. In bed I'd hear him slowly pulling the chains to reset the brass counterweights, that satisfying mechanical clicking. No one but him was permitted to do it. When the clock fell off the wall he gathered the broken pieces and put them in a brown paper shopping bag in the hall closet. The little wooden bird he kept perched on the windowsill in the kitchen. I'm not sure what happened to it. A cuckoo clock, she repeats scornfully. As a wedding gift. I mean, *can you imagine?*

He was nothing like them, she says. I wish you knew him. He was funny, generous. He wasn't a bigot. If he was around they would've never taken what should've been yours.

Best I can tell, their belongings were sold three months ago. The website of Heatherstone Estate Management lists them as clients. I notice on a recent listing that during the last day of a sale, prices drop 10 percent every hour: in the final hour everything is 90 percent off. I admire their refusal to give things away for free. It strikes me as respectful and uncompromising. I used to love yard sales, haggling over jigsaw puzzles with homeowners in their front yards. Sometimes there'd be a dozen guayabera shirts and as many pairs of pants on a clothes rack, a dead man's entire wardrobe. Which used to seem so heartless and grim, but it doesn't anymore. Now I see it as a salutary part of the life cycle. Dissipation. I wish I could've gone to their estate sale. I wouldn't have needed to buy anything, not even things I recognized as his, but I would've liked to have seen who did.

Is it that there's always been some inner poverty, some shortage which might've been solved or explained by him? Children,

I read somewhere, are the living messages we send to a time we will not see. Presently I stand at the window, in the time he cannot see, watching my son juggling a soccer ball in the park across from our house, moving his lips to count each one, trying to break his own record, imagining myself ten years from now recalling this moment, the bittersweetness of the future looking back at the past to infect the present. Remembering lines from a book, or a movie, or maybe a dream: Sometimes I imagine that the dead are allowed to watch their children. This would be one of their privileges. But there must come a point where the dead really wouldn't want to look.

Nights, unable to sleep, I play a solo round of I remember. I remember having my foot measured. I remember carrying money loose in my pocket, back when three or four dollars was so *powerful*. I remember when my future was more interesting to me than my past. Back when I used to dream of being an architect, instead of dreaming of when I used to dream of being an architect. Dreaming ahead not dreaming behind. Before I was pasteurized by balanced meals and chitchat and solvency and fatherhood and the increasing urge and diminishing dexterity to make people laugh. Lately I realize I'm boring somebody and I'll just keep on talking. I want to see how far I can bore into the gray lukewarm center of boring. I think I might find comfort there. I remember raising a hand when the guest speaker asked who in the audience has lost someone to addiction. It wasn't true. I was seated in the front row and for the rest of the talk the speaker gestured to me while making points about addiction, and I nodded back at her with the knowing solemnity of the bereaved.

I remember maps. I remember getting lost. I remember being rewarded just for following along.

I finally pinpoint the buzzing sound, in the living room behind the built-in bookshelves. I move the books and hold my ear to the wall: a constant low hum. I go and inspect the outside wall. No wires or anything electrical, just molting blue stucco lying in scab-like shards around the yard. Underneath blue stucco: bluer stucco. There's a tiny opening by the slab foundation. I watch four, five, six bees fly in and out. They've made our house a hive. Times like this I ask myself: What would you do if you were me? And I give myself permission to do nothing.

My mother mails us all of her dishware and silverware except for two plates, two bowls, two knives, two forks, and two spoons. She mails the jai alai cesta that used to hang with a fern in it in the living room. A money clip of my father's that I've never seen before. The tarnished samovar she bought at a junk sale for six dollars. Hammered brass and always cold to the touch.

Masking tape on the bottom with *family heirloom* written on it. Seriously or sarcastically, I can't tell. She mails ziplock after ziplock of photos. *Still downsizing!* she writes. *Soon I'll be small enough to fit into a suitcase...*

She's stopped going to church. Sometimes she parks in front of a Hindu temple in Port Orange. She calls it the monastery. She says she feels peace wash over her when she idles in the parking lot. It looks like sculpted sugar. She has no desire to go inside or learn about the temple's sacred geometry. That would ruin it. There are peacocks living in the banyan trees out front. People entering with armfuls of fruit and flowers. It's all the religion she needs, she says, this lovely strangeness outside, the void within.

She calls and asks for my son. She tells him to get to the internet, fast. He runs and asks me to use my computer because Grandmére says something's happened. She tells him where to go and he calls out the letters to me, and soon we're looking at a black-and-white live feed of an eagles' nest. The eggs have finally hatched, she tells him. He and I watch. A surly eagle perched astride two eaglets shivering in a crooked bed of twigs. My mother found this site last year—she watched it with her students in class but now keeps it on all day when she's at home. He hands me the phone. How's it going? I ask her. So far so good, she says. I think they'll survive. I meant with you, I say. Look, she says, the father's returned with a fish. I look. The mom starts tearing at flesh and feeding her young. It was alive a second ago, she says. Incredible. One moment you're swimming and the next, bam. You're flying. And then you're dead, I say. I hear her sigh and open the freezer door, grab a handful of ice cubes, drop them into a glass, uncork a bottle, and fill the glass with wine. After a while she says, I think I'd like to be buried at sea.

I remind her that she has a spot in the family plot in Kentucky and she says, I'd rather be ground into dog food.

Sometimes she and him talk on the phone for nearly an hour. When he hangs up he says, I never knew Grandmére was so *interesting*.

She knows he's into drawing, so she mails him sketchpads and sets of markers and pastels. He draws things he thinks she'll like—sunsets, manatees, a self-portrait—and we mail them to her as thank-you cards. For some reason she asks if he believes in God, and he tells her he believes in the gods, like his Greek grandfather, who claims to be a pantheist. He says he prays to Zeus because Zeus is less busy. She loves that. She tells all her friends about it. She starts mailing him books about the gods.

* * *

His favorite stories of mine are from my feckless college days. I tell him about delivering campus mail on a moped, living in a condemned rooming house without electricity, sleeping on an ice-cold waterbed, and waking up one day with hypothermia.

I explain what a waterbed is. And hypothermia. I tell him about the possums that made a den behind a discarded mattress in the hallway. And about selling my plasma. Plasma, I say, is the fluid left over after cells are separated from your blood. I sold my plasma three times a week. I was a Super Donor.

Did it hurt? he asks. Not really, I say, I remember feeling lightheaded afterward.

What else happened? he asks.

I try to remember. I can't tell him about the thing burned deepest into my brain. The guy in the field across from the rooming house, mornings, nights, always in a bathrobe. Always tiptoeing, testing each step as if crossing a cloud. Someone discovered that he was buggering an oak tree at the edge of the field. I guess there was a notch in the trunk. I don't know. After that I despaired for the tree. It looked completely deranged. The town festered. Friday nights a city truck would crawl by, blasting the streets with mosquito-killing poison to get us ready for the weekend, and I'd hold my breath and cover my mouth with whatever fast-food napkins were lying around.

Instead I go on about the plasma center, how they didn't pay you if you passed out before your plasma was extracted.

So we had to work as a team. Yes, it's actually a lesson about teamwork. All of us in our vinyl chairs, we kept watch on each other. Made sure we stayed conscious. When someone sneezed the brief silence afterward would pull at us like the branching limbo before a diagnosis... until all of us called out, Bless you.

Or the summer a professor left me in charge of her house and her rat terrier, Sergei. At night he'd burrow under the covers and lick my toes for an hour while I fell into a brackish sleep. Then one day, out of nowhere, he quit racing to greet me at the door. He wouldn't make eye contact. I couldn't help thinking he'd licked his way into some awful secret knowledge of me. He wouldn't even eat if I was around. I'd give him a biscuit and he held it in his mouth until I left the room.

I rooted through the professor's closets. I read her mail. I had no qualms. The letters were never interesting—if they'd been filled with secrets, I probably would've felt ashamed. It didn't occur to me that this was what I hunted for, something private enough to make me feel terrible for reading it. One envelope contained a department-store credit card. I trashed the envelope and kept the card in my wallet.

At the mall with a friend I saw the pale-blue department-store sign and remembered the card. Two floors of kitchen and bath supplies and high-end women's clothing. It wasn't stealing, I assured him. Insurance would pay for everything. We bought terry-cloth robes, body pillows, muffin tins, a shower radio, a waffle iron. The less necessary, the better. It's absurd, the friend kept repeating. It's *vandalism*. We laughed at the severity of the word.

I dreamed of prison all summer. Alone in a cell plotting my escape. Sometimes it got mixed with the memory of my father in his hospital bed: metal toilet in the corner, gardenias on the nightstand. Him and me locked up together. I'd wake up breathless and grateful. By some miracle clemency, my sentence was commuted. Sergei furiously licking my toes, growling when I reached down to pat him.

Or visiting Cassadaga, a town of fortune tellers. The man studied me with languid intensity and said, Someone has recently died. I told him my father died ten years ago. He said, Ten years is nothing to the dead. He made some other predictions and was wrong about all of them. Still, when he told me I would do something exceptional before I died, I believed him for a long time.

At career day ten parents sit at separate tables in the cafeteria with signs saying what we do for a living. The kids walk around interviewing us. My table starts out busy but word spreads that JoJo's dad, whose sign says FIELD AGENT, is actually a sniper who stands on platforms during Super Bowls aiming his rifle at the crowd. Do you decide when to shoot, or does somebody decide for you? a kid asks. I can't hear the answer. My son is interviewing Avery's dad, the butcher, and I wave and he waves back. What did I expect? Something close to this. What did I hope for? For him to see me in a new light, perhaps, a man with an appreciable career, a specific expertise.

A fourth grader tells me she wants to write a trilogy about cows who escape the slaughterhouse but doesn't know which book to write first. Any advice? Maybe write the first one first, I say. Hmm, she says. She thanks me and goes and asks the butcher the same question.

My mother mails us a box full of shells. Gleaming abalones and clamshells, bleached sand dollars in protective sleeves. I know she's downsizing but the shells look newly bought. Maybe she's thinking: *If they won't move to Florida, I'll move Florida to them.* I await boxes of sandspurs and boxes of sand. Shards of coquina. White hibiscus. A withered grapefruit.

Napping in our empty house, I am awoken by the sound of glass breaking. Silence, then footsteps outside our bedroom. I sit up just as a man opens the door to our room. I see only his chest, shirtless and covered in scratch marks. He takes off running. I chase after him, through the kitchen, outside, before it dawns on me that I have no idea what I'll do if I catch him.

The policeman chastises me for sweeping the broken glass into a pile before he arrives. That's evidence, he says. I follow him through the house. Did you move anything else? he asks. I closed some drawers, picked up books that had fallen off the shelf. He shakes his head. Evidence, he repeats.

He sniffs around the hallway and then lets out a contented sigh. Lean in, he says. Have a whiff. Smell that? Know what it is?

All I'm getting is musty air with some afternotes of police musk, leather, coffee.

Mold? I guess.

Fear, he says with a gleeful croak. It's primitive. Way more primitive than mold.

I don't correct him. I guess he means that fear asserts itself no matter how much perfuming we do. Because it's older than whatever we try to hide it with. Any suspects? I ask, and he says, Yeah, I know exactly who did this. He sounds so certain that for a second I think he means me.

My wife comes home while he's dusting for prints. I tell her what happened, step by step. She tells me I seem strangely excited. I do? I say. You do, the policeman says. Common reaction. It's the adrenaline. Don't worry, he tells my wife, he'll be terrified later. She asks if anything was stolen and the policeman assures her that this particular perp never steals, he only ransacks. He's broken into many other houses around town. He rifles through cabinets, pulls out drawers and empties them onto the floor, kicks the contents from room to room, breaks plates, rearranges pictures on the wall. That's it for now, he says. But guys like this always graduate to more sinister crimes. The policeman tells us about the Golden State Killer's early days as the Visalia Ransacker, then about some other serial killers, he's a bit of a true-crime enthusiast, he says, and I smile because I've heard her rant—she thinks true-crime enthusiasts are as tedious as people obsessed with their genealogy—and he goes on and on until I tell him our son's due home from school soon and we'd like to spare him the sight of his house as a crime scene. The policeman shrugs and finishes his forensics. He carries the evidence away and leaves us to clean the rest.

Terrified yet? my wife asks later. I've been on my computer pricing alarm systems for the last hour, thinking about the ransacker. What would he have done if I wasn't home? Ransacked, sure. But what soft spots would he have exposed? The glass is cleared, the books are shelved, but I still smell traces of fear in the kitchen and hallway, by the bookcase in the living room, on the threshold of our bedroom. I'm a little shaken, but it's not the pure manic fear of childhood. Now it's a gradual movement, like drifting into deeper water unknowingly until you try to touch bottom. Showering before bed I find a strange dark smudge on my thigh. Big, purplish, and circular with an angry, darker off-center eye like Jupiter. I scrub at it as you would a temporary tattoo, but nothing happens.

* * *

I can't sleep. I hold a finger to my wrist and count my resting heart rate. Every website agrees: it's unusual. Sleep used to be so easy, a calm spring warmed by humming turbines… now sleep is a panicked rabbit I clutch tight to my chest. Just keep still and I won't hurt you, I tell my rabbit, but you can't calm the thing you're clutching. I try to tire myself out by plotting and replotting my jogging circuit for tomorrow. Seventh to Mountain, Mountain to Baseline, Baseline to Mills, Mills to Bonita… I wake up exhausted.

Another package arrives, addressed to me. Inside is an omelet pan. I didn't order it. Neither did my wife. I call customer care and all they'll tell me is that somebody paid for it with a credit card over the phone. Who? She won't say. I call my mother: she didn't order it either. I know it's some kind of coded message, and for some reason it scares me more than waking up to a stranger's footsteps. What does it mean? My wife says it couldn't possibly have anything to do with the break-in, unless he planned it weeks in advance—and who sends an omelet pan as a threat? I don't know. Cars drive by the house, slow down, see me looking out the window, speed off. Someone calls and hangs up when I answer. A man in the park does tai chi for a suspiciously long time. I cancel my order for the cheap do-it-yourself alarm system and call a local guy known as the da Vinci of home alarm installation. For now I stack plates by the back door so we'll hear the ransacker if he returns. I put the omelet pan in the garage, where it can't hurt anybody.

They catch him a few days later. He makes the mistake of breaking into a house with a real alarm system, not just a sign out front. The police find him pouring flour and oil onto the kitchen tile. Everyone's talking about it on the neighborhood forum. *Was he making pancakes??* a neighbor writes. Then further down: *I heard he was caught masturbating in Marjory's old bungalow on Seventh and ran away.* Followed by stunned and disgusted emojis by other neighbors. So now I have to make an account and talk to my neighbors. *Thanks for clearing that up!* they say when I assure them the ransacker didn't masturbate in Marjory's old bungalow. *Welcome to our little forum!* they say. *Be sure to sign up for the Labor Day potluck!*

My mother mails us dish towels and extension cords and a forty-year-old blender. A pair of tiny handmade wooden shoes that her mother wore as a child in France. Lacquered, useless, perfect. A saltshaker. *Thinking of china*, she writes. I don't know whether she means the country or the porcelain. Of going there or giving it away.

* * *

She sends a down payment to the Neptune Society. After she dies her ashes will be mixed with concrete and dropped into a memorial reef three miles off the coast of Key Biscayne. That way, she says, you can think about me when you're near the ocean.

I tell her that I'd rather think about the ocean when I'm near the ocean. She ignores me. Back when I got food poisoning on that wretched cruise, she says, I'd lie in bed and feel myself rocking and I realized it was my body getting used to being dead, preparing me. It made me feel better. Then I thought: *You're not rocking, the boat is, the ocean is, you're part of a larger movement*, and even though it probably doesn't seem all that profound to you, it was enormously comforting. The idea of joining the water. Soon. Not tomorrow or next week, but soon.

I follow the alarm guy from room to room. He says home security is mostly a matter of awareness. He says most victims are unwitting and most crimes are crimes of opportunity. He shows me low-vis entry points, tells me I need to trim the bush by the front window. While he pokes his head in the attic, he tells me about a client of his in the foothills. One day things started to go missing: leftovers in the refrigerator, lamps, pillows. He had a ten-thousand-dollar alarm system, the alarm guy says. I inspected it. Checked everything. It was working perfect. Had to be an inside job. Then it hit me. I checked the attic. There he was. He'd been up there for months. How are you gonna keep someone out of your house when he's already in your house?

I bring the omelet pan to class to talk about fear and the uncanny. The scariest details, I say, are often the most unexpected. My students do not agree. They list all the things that are scarier than an omelet pan. Knives, guns, hammers, chains, hooks, blood, teeth, tongues, sharks, bears, pigs, birds, heights, ghosts, twins, rust, lawn mowers, fog, marching bands, zombies, traffic, bacteria, a doctor with normal clothes peeking out of his doctor clothes, the sun. Brian Torres says he'd have a hard time coming up with something *less* scary than an omelet pan. Maybe a bunny. Emma Hughes says, No way. Bunnies are living things. They can be rabid. They can be possessed by demons.

Wait, I know, she says. A *smaller* omelet pan. Everyone laughs.

Mike Adelia, an elderly student who rarely speaks, chimes in. Stories make their own logic, he says. For the writer and the reader both.

Well put, Mike, I tell him.

I'm just quoting you, brother, he says. It's the only thing I've written down all semester.

We drive past a crow pinned to the road, flapping one wing and feebly attempting to take flight. My son wants me to turn around to see if we can help it but I keep driving, thinking that some distance is all he needs to forget. Maybe it is. He doesn't mention the bird again.

I tell him I want to go camping, just him and me. It can be our new tradition. He reminds me that he's afraid of snakes and coyotes, so we end up camping in our backyard. We pitch a tent and lay out sleeping bags and eat soup from cans while waiting for the sun to set. He says, What we're doing—this is camping? Yes, I tell him. Camping's just sleeping outside.

Oh, he says.

He must have imagined something more exotic, like I did when I was his age. Backpacking into the Yukon with my dad, building a lean-to, getting lost while panning for gold and happening upon a pack of bears who protect me and teach me to survive, and when my father returns years later to plant a tree in memoriam we meet again, but I tell him to go home because there's going to be trouble, but he doesn't understand and then I realize I've forgotten my native language and now speak only the bear tongue. He, my son, probably thought we'd at least have a fire.

Don't forget to brush your teeth, my wife calls from the kitchen window.

If I ever went camping with my father I don't remember it. I have a hazy memory of watching some bears fight over trash at the dump, but I might have seen that in a movie.

We aren't brushing our teeth tonight, I tell my son after she closes the window.

On a hike he says, So this is hiking? I tell him hiking's just walking uphill. Oh, he says.

Who knows why I didn't turn the car around when we saw the crow. Whether it was to save him from the sadness of lost causes or simple impatience to get home. Or to teach him that certain things demand his sympathy while other things, most things, do not.

My wife says sympathy isn't like a tank of gas—he's not going to run out of it. I know she's right. Years ago she would ask him, Where's the moon? and he'd look up and find the moon in the night sky and point to it. Always centering his orbit, trying to make what's knowable known.

He knows about the ransacker but not that he entered our house. For now he experiences his parents' anxieties like bad weather: he closes his windows, waits for it to pass. He hasn't yet entered a world where bad things happen to good people, or to bad people. I tell him the riddle of the plane crashing on the border between two countries and I ask where the survivors are buried.

He says without hesitation: In a hideout.

When I tell him you don't bury survivors, he says, They're in a secret hideout.

My mother mails a Polaroid of my father sitting in his faux-leather recliner a few weeks before he died. Stricken, emaciated in a green bathrobe, but smiling as brightly as I've ever seen him smile. Looking at it makes my stomach churn. *Didn't have the heart to throw this away*, she writes. She doesn't add the unspoken question: *Do you?*

A retired preacher sends me an email. She's a former student, the one who wore evening gloves to class and called her classmates idiots for thinking that her memoir, starring a wise and beautiful retired preacher, was supposed to be funny. When I mildly chastised her for it, she asked to speak to my manager. It infuriated me. I yelled at her in class, told her this isn't Burger King. I don't have a manager. Your *chair* then, she said. Is that what you call your manager?

The retired preacher wants me to know that she read one of my stories and wasn't impressed. *What a docile little thing*, she writes in the email. *To your students, you appear to be a rebel with a cause. I dared to ask, What cause? You'd do well to quit writing such mundane stories and turn your pen into a razor and slice the eyes of your reader.*

* * *

Our son wakes us up because he hears noises outside his window. I tell him everything's okay and go into his room with him and pull up the blinds to show him. There in our front yard are three ecstatic-looking coyotes devouring a cat. The coyotes in our town are not noble mascots—they look like starved and hunted dogs. I pull the blinds back down.

Why are they doing that? he asks after he stops crying.

They'll starve to death if they don't, I tell him. But at least Wendy's okay, right?

I find her and bring her into his room and he is still not consoled. I wake up before sunrise to shovel and bag up the leftover mess, hoping he won't remember what he saw. But when I look at his window he's staring out at me, making the moment indelible. Big sleepless man in a bathrobe and kitchen gloves. Who is now implicated in last night's slaughter. I'm the murder explainer, the human helper.

Why haven't I ever seen you cry? he asks me later that day.

I watch him sleep, stand over his bed like a ghost haunting the remains of my old life, too stubborn and attached to pass into the next world. I watch until it feels like I'm an intruder. One night, he starts laughing in his sleep, laughing so hard he wakes himself up. Can you imagine? When he opens his eyes he sees me standing there. He doesn't ask what I'm doing. He just closes his eyes on me. And I am gone.

* * *

Four years left when he was my age now, three years left, two. My son draws my portrait for Father's Day. I look a little constipated, fingers hovering above a misshapen laptop. *You were a good dad*, it says.

There are things I know I should be teaching him and showing him: truths, values, important concepts. I teach him how to draw a horse. I point to trees and say their names. His mother unearths her trumpet from the garage and plays scales for him, shows him how to blow into the mouthpiece. We foster, we abet, we kindle. On Saturdays I fling myself around the local skate park with a colleague's teenage son. One day he cancels because he has to take the PSAT so my son joins me instead. He's never seemed interested in skateboarding, and I haven't wanted to impose it on him. I started soon after my father died, after quitting swim team and baseball and everything else, and what I liked most was that it wasn't corrupted by coaches and parents. No one keeping score or timing me or yelling from the bleachers.

We start in the parking lot. I name each part of the skateboard: nose, tail, grip tape, wheels, bearings, trucks. I hold his hands as he tries to balance. Right foot here, I say, and put your left below the truck bolts, lean forward, bend your knees. I'm letting go now. Ready? He rolls a few feet and slips out and falls. Not hard, but the sudden punishment for being off-balance always comes as a jolt. Now it can go one of two ways: either he asks to go home or he tries again. He stands up. He changes his stance on the board, from regular to goofy, and coasts a little farther.

I take him to the skate shop for a board. The kid working there presents him with choices: Antihero or Welcome, Thunder or Venture, Spitfire or Bones. Mob or Jessup. I remember back when I started, this thrilling new arcane vocabulary. Trick names like a cipher to decode, pro skaters with names like secret identities: Neil Blender, Lance Mountain, Billy Ruff. Sometimes while driving around I get a glimpse of a particular kind of California sunlight I remember from skate magazines, a murky yellow glow I didn't realize was endemic as I pored over photos and their captions: *Natas Kaupas, ollie footplant, Santa Monica.*

We go to the skate park every Saturday, then Saturday and Sunday, and then every day after school. Often I drop him off and read student work in the park. I'm within reach but not overbearing, present but out of sight. Like my own father. Like Jesus. I drive him and his friends to Encinitas, comforted by the familiar chatter in the car about which skater did what trick on which handrail. I tell them about driving to far-flung cities around Florida to skate drainage ditches and marble ledges, about the after-hours skate park inside the roller rink, about the kid who'd follow you around and land whatever trick you were trying, and how this and many other things were *illegal*. Certain words and tricks and clothing, and it was ever-changing. I tell them about my ill-fated trip to EMB in San Francisco and about the backyard vert ramp whose owner wouldn't let kids skate unless they dropped in from the top. I was the first of my friends to try and I fell ten feet straight to the flat bottom and was knocked cold. My friends took turns describing the sound: moose hit by truck, ham dropped from helicopter. Later I tried again and fell just as hard. I could barely walk. I didn't tell my mother because I was afraid she'd make me quit. All week I worked out what I had to do different: lean forward, squat lower. I went back but the owner wouldn't let me try it again—he was worried I'd sue him. I know there's a point here. Something about persistence, or idiotic determination. But I'm not sure the lesson's coming through. Or if it needs to. I'm starting to suspect that the point is often beside the point.

Skateboarding is not a metaphor. Still, listening to him in the driveway, spending hours trying to land a kickflip, the surge of joy I feel is so strong and uncorruptible I can hardly abide it.

* * *

I rent a van on his thirteenth birthday and drive him and his friends to a skate park in Simi Valley. I film them skating and send their parents the clips. A local pro shows up and I tell him it's my son's birthday and he gives him a pair of shoes and socks with weed leaves on them. On the way home they're all teasing each other about the stupid things they were interested in before skateboarding. Pokémon, soccer, reading. My son says he doesn't remember. I do, I say. I tell them how much he loved Peter Pan. It's all he wanted to watch—one Halloween we made him a Peter Pan costume and he wore it for months. Until the feather fell off the hat and the pants disintegrated in the wash. His friends shriek with laughter. He reenacted the movie from memory, I say, scene by scene. Our dog was Wendy. I spent weeks editing the video. We still have it. Oh my god, they say. We *need* to see that.

Stop it, my son hisses at me in the passenger seat.

Years from now I'll think of this moment not as the end but as a beginning. A growing self-consciousness in him, perfectly natural, a need for discernible boundaries. And a start to me stumbling through where to align myself between friend and caretaker. He used to say he wished I was his age so I didn't have to work and we could hang out and draw and make movies all day long. The problem: I wished that too. It's been a long time since he's told me that. He has secrets. He thinks things he doesn't say. Where are you going? I say when I hear him at the front door. Down to Baja, he says, a callback to a joke of mine that he never found funny.

His next birthday I drop him and some friends off at Raging Waters and reserve a rideshare home for them. My wife and I eat lunch at a neighbor's house. We sit around a firepit in their backyard, talking the way you do with people you don't know too well, airing our neutral opinions with conviction, airing our convictions neutrally. I go home and sulk. I leaf through old photo albums. I drink a beer and try to bleed myself of nostalgia. From the front window I see the exterminator pull up in his whiskered white truck. He's here to kill the ants that have veered off from the mega colony on the coast. When he's done he calls out, See you next year, and waves to me with the wand of his poison sprayer.

Children are the living messages. Maybe that's the problem. Something got lost between my father and me and me and my son. The baton dropped. Maybe the only reason I still write about him is in the hopes of finally getting it right. So I can be done with it and write something else. Finding a direct line, one that isn't just a summary of a retelling of a memory of a truer story. The combination of words that closes the door behind me and draws a path to whatever's next.

* * *

I remember weekend mornings our son used to crawl into bed with us and lie with his back flat to my chest. He was impossibly warm. Ever since he was an infant he loved lying atop me, and ever since he was an infant I thought the same thing when he did it: I am the grave. You are the marker.

The robins never return to my office. The eggs go gray but I leave the nest where it is. My students ask about it and I tell them what happened, doing my best not to turn it into a lesson. I quit quoting other writers to them. I won't even say the name Flaubert out loud anymore. I quit claiming all stories are love stories. Or ghost stories. Or detective stories. I have a colonoscopy, two root canals, a tetanus shot, hernia surgery. A guy in a beekeeper suit cuts into our stucco wall and loads bees and honeycomb into pickle buckets, showing them to me in the window before he loads them onto his truck. Five buckets of bees. We're off to Bakersfield, he says. A friend joins a peyote church. The trees marked with X's are chopped down, their trunks pulled up at the roots, and new trees are planted in their place. A neighborhood couple's decision to swap partners ends predictably. I buy an air purifier. I buy a Soviet-era watch. I fly to Florida to help my mother move into a retirement home. We sort through the little she has left: her belongings fit into the trunk and back seat of my rental car. On the way there she says,

It must be hard to see me get old, a moment of insight that silences me. She says, I hope this place isn't full of Republicans. I drive along the beachside, past mounds of rubble where hotels used to be, past the strip club where three of the 9/11 hijackers spent their last night on earth, past Sensei Duane's dojo, long gone, which now houses something called an aggression room where you can pay four dollars per minute to smash things. Stopped at a red light, I recognize a face on a billboard: it's one of the kids who killed the alligator. Joshua Elton. He's a personal injury lawyer now. You cunt, I say out loud. I wonder if he thinks about that day, or if it isn't even close to the worst thing he's done. I go back to California.

My son gets his braces off. His curfew is an hour later than last year. He stops asking me questions he doesn't know the answer to. I stop asking if he wants me to drive him to a skate park in Rialto, La Cañada, El Sereno. I pretend to write a children's book. I pretend to write a postapocalyptic novel. I pretend to write a screenplay. A neighbor has a heart attack while trying to unlock his toolshed. My mother starts forgetting things.

For his birthday we buy him two weeks at a summer skate camp in Pennsylvania. He and I fly out and high-five our good-byes and then I drive a rented Kia around the Midwest seeing friends. On the way to Indianapolis I get a call from my old grad school friend whom I was going to stay with. His daughter has pneumonia. Can we meet for a quick beer instead? I'm on the outskirts of Canton, two hundred miles away. I've just been to the Football Hall of Fame and have emerged oddly inflated. Ready to block a punt or ruin my body for a grizzled old coach I begrudgingly love. I tell him we'll do it some other time, and head south, around Dayton and past Cincinnati, into Louisville. I spend the night at a Red Roof Inn.

All night long I'm awoken by a phone ringing in the room next door, its frenetic ringtone a perfect imitation of a phone going insane. It rings again before sunrise and I realize it's coming from my room. I find the phone wedged between the wall and the headboard. I pause—this is how action movies begin—and finally answer. The caller apologizes. She says she's outside my door. I open it and hand her the phone.

I don't know what I'm doing in Kentucky. I thought maybe I'd go to a Sunday service at my aunt and grandmother's church, but when I open the blinds I see it's raining hard and my plan, flimsy to begin with, collapses. I eat a gas station banana and a gas station orange and watch my third-favorite Sylvester Stallone movie on TV. I call my wife. I call my son—he's using his phone to film him and his fellow campers skating the A-frame. And he's almost out of battery. So he has to go. Be careful, I say and he says yep. Send me a clip, I say, and he says, Gotta go, and ends the call.

When the rain lets up I drive around. Over the years, without exactly intending to, I've gotten really good at driving, intuiting my way through traffic, switching from offense to defense, foreseeing the unforeseeable. I enjoy it. I find it calming, stimulating even, which I suspect is an indication of a simple mind. Past the family cemetery, the mall, their old house, children's bikes and balls out front. The acre plot of land where my grandfather kept a garden. Thinking nothing as I drive past, nothing but: I remember, I remember, I remember.

Before leaving town I text my cousin Rusty. He tells me to meet him at a bar called The Outlook. He shows up forty-five minutes late. I've had two drinks and am unabashedly happy to see him. Clogged fucking fuel filter, he says. His hair is gray at the sides, and he's put on some weight—he looks how I imagine my father might've looked in his fifties. He orders a shot of bourbon and a Bud Red, which turns out is just normal Budweiser, and skips the small talk to tell me what he's angriest about. Before she died Aunt Freddie promised him her 300ZX—glacier white, no rust, low miles—but ended up giving it to the church with everything else. Now he sees a fat deacon driving it around town. It's probably his third car.

Did you get a bear? I ask.

Those special-needs bears? he says. I put them out of their misery. He says he stole some boxes from their garage before the estate sale but it was mostly junk, old tax forms and knickknacks and Christmas ornaments. Those dickheads loved Christmas, he says. Those things should've been ours, he says. We're family. I cleaned their goddamn rain gutters. In the sun. For free.

I try to work up some outrage, but it's been too long. I ask about his daughter, who's in college. Talking about her disarms him. He's proud, spiteless, sentimental. She plays volleyball. She wants to be a dentist. How about your son? he says. I give my three-sentence roundup: skateboarding, school, art. I show him pictures. I say it's strange. I thought raising an infant would be hard and it'd get easier but it's the opposite. I have no clue what I'm doing.

Nobody does. My method is, think about what my father would do… then do something different. Hasn't steered me wrong yet.

His smile is like a wince. He orders another shot of bourbon. I bet he's just like you, he says. Probably not as fucked up.

Fucked up?

You were a wreck. Always mumbling to yourself, zipper down, shoes untied. Wearing a pin that said the Butthole Suffers.

Surfers. It was a band.

Sure.

Was my zipper down a lot?

Your granny thought the devil had you. She was praying for Jesus to give you mouth-to-mouth.

He says he has something for me but he left it out in the car. I wait, fully prepared to never see him again. A Scorpions song plays for the third time, the one with all the hopeful whistling. Rusty finally returns smelling like cigarette smoke and holding a small gray plastic notebook.

I found it in one of the boxes, he says. I've looked at it a few times and I'm still not sure what to make of it. I'm pretty sure it belonged to your dad.

The bartender sets the shot in front of Rusty, who picks it up, sniffs it delicately, and sets it back down.

It's crazy, he says. I mean, look at you. Never in a million years would I have guessed you'd turn out so…

What?

Normal, he says.

3.

OWLS

Father and son loading the car at dawn. Father loading the car, son in the passenger seat wedging a pillow against the window in hopes of salvaging a few more minutes of sleep. Father notices a red-tailed hawk in the park across the street, strutting in the grass, scrounging for bugs like some common yardbird. It fills him with a muddled feeling he isn't sure what to do with. Bury it then, pray it stays in the ground. Mother in the window waving goodbye.

The morning air smells liked burnt fruit. Fire danger: extreme. Traffic: backed up near Azusa by a jettisoned mattress. News helicopter: stalled aloft like a dragonfly in a jar. The mountains glow orange as if lit from within. The effect of the morning light on the mountains, the glow, is called alpenglow. Father can't remember if he's told his son this. Should he now? Should he point it out as if he's never told him, or phrase it like a question, or make a joke of it? Well, son, you've reached the age when you're ready to know the German words for things. Seems like only yesterday when my own father sat me down and told me about the zeitgeist...

Son slumps in the passenger seat, earbuds in, eyes closed. He stirs awake every few minutes and types something into his phone. Father wants to imagine him keeping a detailed log of what he's thinking and remembering but he's probably texting his ex-girlfriend how much he misses her already.

The blitzkrieg? The schadenfreude?

Who is this? son says, removing one of his earbuds and nodding to the radio. Father tells him the Kinks. Sunny Afternoon. It was one of the son's favorite songs when he was very young, before he had favorites of his own, but father knows it's tedious to remind sons how much they used to love certain things.

Sounds like circus music, he says, replacing the earbud.

You used to love this song, father says.

They're driving to Los Angeles. After Los Angeles they'll head north, like father's father did forty years ago, following his path, city by city, step by step.

I probably used to love clowns too, son says.

Between them in the center console sits the gray book, palm-sized with a laminated cover and lined paper yellowing at the edges. Father's been the keeper of it since that night in

Kentucky when he and Rusty parted with a clumsy hug and he read it under the dome light in his rental car and again in the motel.

March 1978. His father flew from Florida to Los Angeles alone, drove up the coast, waded in the ocean, visited a castle, drank beer, met people, ate dim sum, went to Alcatraz, and returned eleven days later. The gray book is a record of that trip, a letter from the grave in meticulous block letters.

A letter from the grave? That sounds promising! It's full of advice then? And fatherly wisdom?

No, neither. The notes are cryptic, perfunctory, repetitive, obsessive about driving times and how much things cost. The father—the son, that is, the father's son... I mean *me*—I can't even decode a lot of it.

Landed in LA. Haze. Thrifty, Ford Granada, $116. Pear in the GC.

I've had it three years. I've shown it to family and friends hoping they'll see something I don't. They leaf through it and hand it back with a shrug. I asked my mother about it. I brought it to my creative writing class. I read the first entry and asked, What's the story here? No response. What can we deduce from his notes?

A man flew to Los Angeles, a student said.

And rented a car, another added. For a hundred and sixteen dollars.

A torpor fell over the room. Spontaneous protective hibernation. It happens when they sense that my point is not going to be worth the work it takes to arrive at it.

The pear in the GC? I said to the only student looking at me. Thoughts on the pear?

No one had thoughts on the pear. Then Jimmy Escalera raised his hand to tell us that his grandfather kept a journal in Vietnam. There were Bible verses and parts of it were written in code. Certain pages had tally marks at the top and these, Jimmy was pretty sure, stood for the people his grandfather killed.

Vietnam, secret code, tally marks. Everyone agreed there was a story here.

When you can't decipher a sound you move closer to it. That's my thinking. Plus my son leaves for college at the end of summer. The road is where fathers and sons bond. It's where they stare meaningfully into the horizon and think things and say them.

He sits around all day watching cartoons, Jimmy Escalera said in class. Without the journal we'd never know he used to be a killing machine.

I couldn't sleep last night. I never can before a trip. I lay in bed trying to arrange my feelings into something like a viewpoint as coyotes yipped and yawped outside. My wife tries to temper my expectations. Focus on him, she says, meaning our son. Keep it fun. Don't get all impatient or morose. Her advice is reasonable. This isn't a quest. I have a route, hotel reservations, six apples, my son in the passenger seat. I have ideas, cobbled from movies and books and pharmaceutical ads, about road trips, fathers, sons, the ocean, self-discovery, messages, buried in notes and letters, hidden for years. I fell asleep charting our route, conceiving scenarios sentimental enough to make a pig blush. Standing atop a cliff in Big Sur and hearing his voice, driving up the coast and finding closure, et cetera. I dreamed of running through the woods toward a faraway light. I woke up before reaching it. Cotton-mouthed, legs sore from the idea of running. I studied myself in the mirror as I brushed my teeth: droopy eyes, sharp nose. Face of a steamed turtle. Still hazily devising scenarios: touring Alcatraz and realizing things, eating dim sum and coming to terms. Yearning for something big and decisive, knowing it's a deluded feeling and yet feeling it strongly.

Santa Anita: infield passes, pond oysters. Drunks from Phx. Mutual man says GR way up.

My son reads this aloud as we approach the exit for Santa Anita Park. We pull off and drive along streets lined with towering palms and into the racetrack parking lot, which is empty. The gates were supposed to open a half hour ago. I flag down a woman in a golf cart and ask her what's going on. She says she isn't sure. She has no connection to the track, she's just driving her golf cart through the parking lot.

On his phone my son discovers Santa Anita closed after the twenty-seventh horse died this racing year. People are sad, people are angry, but no one can agree on why the horses died. It could be simple negligence. Or drugs. Or rainfall from an atmospheric river that flooded the turf. It could be a man named Felix Concepción, who trained eight of the fallen horses.

That place sucks, my son says as we merge onto the highway. I hope it stays closed.

I make affirming noises. I tell him people are predicting the death of horse racing. Like dog racing and indoor smoking and the set shot in basketball. I imagine my father, ninety years old this year, sitting in his faux-leather recliner, watching the things he knew so well wink out of existence. I know horse racing is inhumane, unnecessary, and I doubt I'll ever visit another track again, but I'll be sad to see it go. Tolerably sad, like when you find out someone you thought already died has died.

I tell my son what I remember about the track where my father worked: gamblers and their morning cigars, shredded bits of money on the floor of the betting windows, from cashiers pulling the rubber bands off the bundles. My father gave them to me. Old pennies too. I collected pennies and torn bits of money. It sounds like a Depression-era childhood. Your grandfather fell in love with horses and numbers in college, I say. It's where you get your talent for math.

What'd he do with numbers? he asks.

Calculated odds, I say. Or payouts based on the odds. He calculated something.

Didn't they have calculators?

You know, it's possible he didn't calculate anything, I say. Maybe he just liked being around them. Numbers.

A few years ago I found out my father needed just one elective class to graduate from college but never ended up taking it. I tell my son this and he says, That's cool.

You would've liked him, I say. Another bland, untrue thing. I want to strike it out the second it leaves my mouth.

What's seventy-seven times seventeen? I ask a few miles later.

I'm tired, Dad. Then, a minute later: One thousand three hundred and nine.

I was five when my father flew to California. I have no memory of him being gone. I shouldn't be surprised that he doesn't mention me in the gray book. What would he have written? There wasn't much to me at age five. I liked garbage trucks. I liked candy. Most of my dreams were about animals.

He doesn't mention any trees or birds or premonitions or songs. Or his wife. So I shouldn't be surprised. But it bothers me. I've flipped through the book a hundred times and I still catch myself hoping to find something that's not there.

* * *

GP Observatory. James Dean, planetarium. Barely see Hollywood sign. Oxygen balloon, stepped in gum.

That's it? my son says after I read the entry. We've parked and walked up the hill and are standing outside the Observatory.

Yeah, I say. That's all he had to say about Griffith Park.

Basic, he says.

Miles south, patches of smog shroud the downtown skyline like scum on stew. Hollywood sign. Planetarium. It's all here. Even James Dean's seductive head, mounted to a pillar in bronze. We're near the spot in Rebel Without a Cause where Plato asks him, You think the end of the world will come at nighttime, Jim? And he answers forlornly: At dawn.

My son asks why my father came to California alone. I wondered the same thing, I tell him. My mother said it was probably a work trip. Plus, she added, families didn't fly cross-country willy-nilly back then. At least ours didn't.

Could be he had a second family, he says.

Could be, I say. Oxygen balloon. What's an oxygen balloon?

He types it into his phone. He scrolls and scrolls, looking for a satisfactory result. He probably meant helium, he says.

He wanders off to the gift shop to buy his ex-girlfriend a souvenir. A young couple asks if I can take their picture next to James Dean's head and I oblige. I rarely feel as useful as when

I'm taking a stranger's picture for them. I zoom out and zoom in, milking it longer than I need to. When I'm done the man extends his fist, and I bump it with mine and return his phone with the other hand, and our exchange happily concludes.

My son and wife and I used to visit the Observatory once a year. I don't remember why we stopped—whether we got bored of it or he did. We should've continued coming here, I think. We shouldn't have let boredom stop us.

He returns with a solar system bracelet for his ex-girlfriend. Seeing all those hopeful colored orbs dims my mood.

Nice bracelet, I tell him.

Are we done? he asks.

A lap around the planetarium, another stop at James Dean's head. A passable likeness but up close I notice he has no eyes. *It ended with his body changed to light*, says the inscription. I like that. I write it down. I look west. I think about oxygen. I scan the ground for gum. I open the gray book and read the entry one more time. Anything? Anything? Nothing. I might as well try to manufacture a sneeze. I take another lap and head back to the car.

We used to park by the zoo and see the koala before P-22, the wild mountain lion living in Griffith Park, mauled and ate him. Maybe that's why we quit coming. We visited the koala then hiked up to the planetarium and reclined and watched a light-show rendition of the birth of the universe with disco sound effects. The universe was created in 1977, my wife would say, and I would laugh and he would laugh because I laughed. We'd walk out giddy, veneered with sound and light. We'd eat potpies at a Vietnamese restaurant in Glendale. I don't know why it served potpies but everyone ordered them. We brought colored pencils with us because the potpies took forty-five minutes to make. He'd draw on his place mat and then ours, whatever heroic figure he was obsessed with at the time: Apollo, Peter Pan, Didier Drogba. He could busy himself for hours conjuring and reconjuring it. We still have giant plastic bins full of his drawings in our garage. And those intricate hand-drawn mazes he made after he stopped drawing—he'd give me one and I would work my way in and out of it before realizing there was no solution. Getting lost was the point, or there was no point. The only way to solve it was to turn back around and exit the same way you entered.

We drive in silence, into the smog and stew. I try to quiet my mind. Nature preserve, I say when we pass a nature preserve. Motivate Hollywood, I say when we pass a sign that says MOTIVATE HOLLYWOOD. I point out the site of the hotel where Bobby Kennedy was killed, now a twenty-four-hour gym. There's Forest Lawn, where Michael Jackson and his chimpanzee are buried. I tell him that the man who built Forest Lawn wanted to make a cemetery like a beautiful park where families would picnic and frolic around their dead loved ones. He thought cemeteries were too sad.

My son scrolls through his phone. He says it's true that Michael Jackson is buried there, but Bubbles the chimpanzee is still alive and living in Florida. Is he happy? Does he miss Neverland? It doesn't say. But you can visit the sanctuary where he lives, about an hour's drive from where I grew up.

I'm sending Grandmére a link, he says. She loves stuff like this.

Really? I thought animals annoyed her.

Don't you remember the nest cam? The dolphins behind her condo?

Yeah.

The panda cam.

Okay, you're right. (I forgot about the panda cam.) She's an animal lover.

It says he goes totally berserk if he hears a Michael Jackson song. Even someone humming it. It's too painful. He doesn't want to be reminded.

My wife had to talk him into coming on this trip. I didn't hear the conversation but I can imagine—I'll spare you the reenactment. I don't blame him. I haven't been good company lately. I've been fretting over my own extinction again. Blood tests, midnight trips to the emergency room, the whole opera.

One of my tumors turned out to be a sinus infection. Another was a hernia. I can hardly look my doctor in the eye anymore. There's pity in her gaze, sure, and something truer and meaner, beneath pity.

I see what she sees: craven insoluble fear. I can marinate in it or try to dull it with a glass of wine or two, usually two, maybe three, rarely four, sometimes four, never five, almost never, and how much is a glass anyway?, it's an arbitrary measure, and then I'm playing photo roulette on my computer again—think of a date then find a picture as close to it as possible—January 25, 2006, deep winter, Iowa City, our son and a friend bundled up on a freezing train ride by the river, him in his tiny red snow boots, studying the picture then spelunking into the garage through plastic bins to find the boots, I want to hold them for a second, and my son opens the garage door with the remote to pull the car in and sees me, playfully taps the horn, and says, What are you doing, bro?, yes, here he is in the flesh, out of the car, taller than me even though he's two inches shorter than me, and I feel so chaotic and stilted around him sometimes, like now, and I say, The garage is filthy, bro, and he heads inside without us saying a single meaningful thing to each other, I know I can't go on like this, and I keep looking for his boots but can't find them. Instead I content myself with his Peter Pan costume. I don't caress it against my cheek with tears in my eyes or anything. I'm not a sociopath. I just look at it. I'm spiraling. I have to *do* something. Which is as close as I have come to a plan. Stop spiraling, do something. So something is exactly what I'm doing.

My reenactment involves my wife detailing all the reasons why he should join me, then offering to pay him, and him holding out for more money. I have no evidence, just a gut feeling. Something about how he sits next to me in the car, biding his time like he knows the meter's running.

My mother calls. The phone rings in a different language when you know you're not going to answer it.
    Why aren't you picking up? he says.

My mother cut back on her drinking in her seventies, read a book a week, went to New Zealand, gave away any possession she didn't use at least once a week except for a grapefruit spoon and a black clambroth marble that reminded her of one she had as a girl. She started fostering retired racing greyhounds. She fostered three of them until she realized it made her too sad. Not parting with them but the dogs themselves, their spindly bodies and meek sensitive faces, which seemed to exude judgment by withholding it. They were like hobbled horses, pinioned birds. She bought two feeders instead, filled them with nectar, hung them on her back porch.

She entered her eighties bright and lucid but now, four years on, she's begun to flicker. She's drinking in the mornings again. When we talk on the phone, especially after she's had a few glasses of wine, we end up arguing over some stupid point of fact. The specifics aren't important, she tells me when I correct her for confusing the recent past and the distant past. I know I should stop correcting her. She still has her hair done once a week. She still gets annoyed when someone doesn't bless her after she sneezes. And recently she met a man in the retirement home. His name's Elias Parker. They eat dinner together every day, then watch old movies in the TV room. She thinks they're in love. She says they went to high school together, but he looks about ten years older than her and has a vaguely Hungarian accent.

The other day she called to ask if I remembered the girl who lived next door. Not next door to the town house where I grew up but next to the beachside duplex where my mother grew up. Beautiful jet-black hair down to the small of her back, she said. Her father punished her by cutting it off. Remember? Remember how we all cried?

When I read to her from the gray book or ask her about some name, she tells me to quit interrogating her. He's been dead longer than he was alive, she says.

Not yet, I tell her. Four more years.

See, I don't think it's normal that you know that.

She no longer thinks about him like she used to. She allows herself to remember him while waiting for a bag of popcorn to finish in the microwave. Three minutes and forty seconds, she says. The perfect amount.

Hollywood Blvd.
Addict on sidewalk
Lady with dummy
Chinese preacher
Sax player in diapers
Met people

The Vietnamese restaurant in Glendale is sorry but it's closed for repairs. We go to Philippe's instead where my father might well have eaten forty-five years ago after he went to the Observatory. He might've met people here. We order French dips from a guy with a carving knife, who deftly slices meat onto a hoagie roll. We sit at a long table and eat without talking, father, son, and meat. Next to us two old men are talking about something one of them read in the newspaper. A mall Santa in Upland claims he visited the hospital room of a boy whose last wish was to die on Santa's lap. He held the boy in his arms and described how nice heaven will be, and the boy died right there in his arms. That's what the man alleges. But now no one in the hospital can corroborate his story. So wait, says one of the men in the restaurant. Did Santa Claus kill that boy?

Hmm, my son says, scrolling as I drive.

What? I say.

Nothing.

Tell me. I'm bored.

Ian posted an old picture of a bunch of us at Poods and Benji commented.

The casket kid?

Nobody calls him that anymore. *We look at the world once, in childhood.* That's what Benji wrote. It's probably from a song.

It's from a poem. The rest is memory.

What?

That's the next line.

Yeah. Benji's pretty fried now. He usually just comments with fire emojis. Beach picture, fire emojis. Your dad died, fire emojis.

I bet he enjoys the ambiguity.

Benji forgot his own birthday last year, he says.

When he scrolls through his phone his face bears the expression of someone in love.

Twelve miles west of Burbank, I try to figure out a way to initiate conversation that isn't burdensome or annoying. Combing my brain for scraps of poems to recite and remembering only the one about your mum and dad fucking you up. They may not mean to, but they do. Realizing that the degree to which they fuck you up can be measured by how often you think about them once you've left home. Something just north of never is ideal. Parents are booster rockets, I think, necessary for takeoff but a burden at higher altitudes. I'm starting to wish we were following our own path. Retracing my father's is too literal, like in movies when people talk to tombstones. A high school quarterback in West Texas who just won state wants his father to know, so he leaves the game ball next to the tombstone and says, I hope you're proud, because dead fathers are able to hear you only if you're within five feet of their graves, and sons can't celebrate with their teams like normal sons when there's a dead father somewhere to commune with.

I could ask him to look up what happens to them after takeoff, booster rockets. How are they retrieved, reused? I could ask him to look up the Challenger explosion, Russian space dogs, the Golden Record.

It's the earbuds. If earbuds weren't plugging his ears I could remind him how we used to drive around with him in his car seat until he fell asleep and one time as he nodded off a pair of fire trucks overtook us, sirens blazing, and he stirred awake and my wife followed them for miles and when she lost them he said *again, again,* which he always said when something pleased him or amused him. Once was never enough. I could ask if he's seen any good movies. I could point to a red Triumph Spider Coupe and say *look*. It wouldn't be like talking to a locked door, fashioning sentences into keys.

Then he takes out the earbuds and nestles them into their charger. The silence abides. We could talk about the guys in Philippe's arguing about the boy who asked to die atop Santa. I could ask him if he remembers when he realized Santa didn't exist.

He was seven. He read Santa's letter thanking him for the cookies and noticed it was in my handwriting. He almost admitted he knew but stopped himself and feigned belief for two years because he thought we'd be disappointed he found out. I want to remind him but I won't. He thinks my wife and I mythologize his childhood—we've built a shrine out of only what is sweet and pleasing to us. We forget our experience of his childhood is secondary to his. We have our bouquet of salient moments and he has his. The winter the whole town froze over and I dropped him onto the ice. He swears it's the first time the world came into focus for him. After that he started having dreams I was a werewolf, which he only recently told me. He had them for years. He said he never actually thought I was a werewolf, but I did act strange sometimes. More like an older brother. Those pressure points you taught me? What was up with that?

The Shah? The Crab Claw? You loved it.

Not really. You told me you knew one that would make somebody instantly shit themselves.

I never said that.

You did.

I probably said crap themselves.

It was weird, Dad.

Those were fake. I made them up.

I know.

I took you fishing. Camping. Remember? Trips to skate parks. Managing your soccer team. Typical dad behavior.

Okay, okay.

Parent-teacher conferences. Career day. Thanksgiving fun run.

I'm not saying you were a bad dad.

But.

But...

But what?

Amusing myself at his expense. Pretending I had a second family in Baja California. Going down to Baja, I'd say when I left the house. Embarrassing him accidentally. Embarrassing him on purpose. Standing with other fathers on the touchline of a soccer field, dispirited by the proprietary way they watched their offspring. Praising each other by praising each other's sons. He loved soccer but hated running. He loved the idea of soccer. Sometimes he'd stop playing altogether to stare off at something only he saw.

A father in a pristine salmon polo kept calling him *dude*: Get back on defense, dude. Win the ball, dude.

A tidy jolt of rage each time he said it. At halftime I asked him if he played. He said, Soccer?, and I shook my head and pointed to the polo logo on his shirt. His tongue darted in and out of his mouth as if it were a separate creature, something trying to hide and advertise what was inside.

My son was mortified when he found out. He told me to try to be like other dads: happy, neutral, normal. He said whenever he looked over at me watching him play I was always scowling.

That's just how my face is, I told him.

Being too rigid and too lenient. Saying one thing and doing another. Telling the truth. Telling lies.

Stuck in traffic I think about the graffiti we saw in Oslo: *You aren't in traffic. You are traffic.* I want to adjust it into a mantra. *I'm not in line. I am line. I'm not in Taco Bell. I am Taco Bell.* My son's at the wheel. I admire his driving style: periodic glances at the rearview and side mirrors, earnest grip on the steering wheel. Because he's driving I feel like I can say anything, so I'm babbling. That's the Greek restaurant where Mom talked to Tom Hanks while in line for the bathroom. Huge asshole, I say.

Really? he says.

No, just making sure you're listening. There's Moonshadows, where Mel Gibson got hammered before his anti-Semitic tirade. That's where we met the real Gidget.

I ask about the game he and his friend Justin used to play in the car. Where they'd wave to people and try to get them to wave back.

Oh god, he says. Sweet and sour.

If they waved back you'd say *sweet*. If they didn't you'd say *sour*.

I remember.

I wave to a woman with hair the color of antifreeze, who glances over and then stares rigidly ahead. Sour, I say. I wave to a man in a red Toyota. Sour, I say. To a man in a delivery van. Sweet.

Are you going to be like this the whole trip? my son asks.

I'm not sure, I say. Possibly. I wave to a woman on the back of a motorcycle, who waves back. Sweet.

How does that other poem go. Lose something every day. Accept the fluster of lost… houses? Cities? Keys? I should've memorized more poems when I was younger. I should've learned Sanskrit and cultivated an aura. I'm thinking about poor Benji: seventeen years old and already fried and wistful for childhood. I drove him home from the skate park years ago. He seemed like a sweet kid. His parents ran a mortuary business out of their house, or they lived in an apartment connected to the showroom. I asked if he ever got spooked being around so many coffins. Coffins? he said. What's a coffin? He'd never heard the word in his life. My family sells caskets, he said.

* * *

Los Angeles to Santa Barbara: about 100 miles. Free ice.

Yes, Father, you are correct, the distance between LA and Santa Barbara is about one hundred miles. What about the ocean? Cliffs curving and jutting over violet water? Velvet mesquites, wild bougainvillea? Firepits and rainbow-patterned umbrellas? Any messages from the grave? Thoughts on the future? What about your wife at home drinking afternoon wine with her friend Bunny, wistfully reading out itineraries from cruise brochures, all those ports of call they'll never see?

She calls me ten miles outside Santa Barbara. I let it ring. I'm thinking about a friend whose father taped a list of rules to their refrigerator. *No singing in the house* was at the top. My mother made no rules or demands. When I behaved badly she would say in an aggrieved voice, You need to act like somebody. She never said who. Again she calls as we're entering city limits. I pick up this time. *Finally*, she says, fumbling with the phone. She waits for me to say something. How's it going? I ask. Not good, she tells me. She's in the lobby of the wound clinic waiting to see a doctor. How come you didn't return any of my calls? she asks. Everyone's hiding from me.

I ask why she's at the wound clinic but all she wants to talk about is Elias Parker. Why hasn't he called her back? What's his problem? His niece thinks I'm after his money, do you believe that? Guess what she does for a living?

Nuclear physicist, I say.

She sighs and says, Where do you come up with this stuff? Most people would say teacher. Lawyer. You like putting knots in everything.

What's his daughter do for a living, Mom?

Niece. She owns her own business. She makes internal organs out of cloth. Little stuffed animals. Except organs.

How would I have guessed that?

You're supposed to guess something normal, then I tell you what she really does and we laugh. She releases a long beleaguered breath. The niece, she says, weighs three hundred pounds.

I let her vent. My son is asleep in the passenger seat, missing Santa Barbara's holy afternoon light. Pale gulls drift above the beach. They make flight look like a sad, heavy talent. I tell her I have to go soon and she asks if I'm writing and I say yes, not right this second, but yes, and she says she's been meaning to tell me that she tried to start a book club at the retirement home as an excuse to get everyone to buy my book—she even promised they could meet the author—but no one signed up for it.

* * *

Finally she tells me why she's at the wound clinic: walking to the bathroom in the middle of the night, she sliced her shin on the planter in her bedroom. That stupid cactus, she says. Why's it there? Looking at it gives me such a terrible feeling.

I ask how serious the wound is and she says, Serious enough to end up at the wound clinic. Wouldn't you think a wound clinic would be nice, by the way? This place is not nice. They don't even have a TV.

Hold on, she says. The nurse is calling me. I'm gonna act like I don't hear her.

Talk to the doctor, I say. Call me when you're back. She sighs and says okay... but can you *please* answer my calls from now on?

When Rusty gave me the gray book I read her one of the entries: *Below Presidio. Helped dig. Candy. Good egg.*

No idea, she said.

Helped dig?

Not ringing any bells.

What about good egg?

Yeah. That sounds like your father.

How?

He always liked eggs.

I haven't told her about the trip. She'd say the idea of following his route is kind of morbid, or at least bad luck. She'd say why not visit her instead. Florida has two coasts. We could visit the beach where she saw Elvis. We could see a colony of displaced wolves.

My son opens his eyes and asks where we are. He says he was dreaming about skating in a contest. He kept messing up and could hear me in the crowd, sighing. We're driving up a mountain and I'm watching the road but out of the corner of my eye I can see him staring. Wonder what it could mean, I say. He isn't smiling. Can't be mad at me for something that happened in a dream, I say. Right?

I heard you sighing as you were talking to Grandmére, he says. I think I brought that into sleep with me. He asks, not for the first time, if I'm mad at her and I say no. Then why do I sound like I am?

Long story, I tell him, and he says, Longer than this drive?

We pull off at the Cold Spring Tavern, an old stagecoach stop. The air is cool and clear and it smells like creosote or sagebrush, some nice chaparral smell. We share a basket of fries and watch a woman painstakingly tuning a Dobro. A single metal crutch leans on the chair next to her. If we don't leave now, I say, we're going to have to sit through at least one song. My son shakes his head and says, I knew you were going to say that.

As a punishment for saying something predictable I make us sit through a song. A man in electrician boots joins her and they cover a song I can't place—the O'Jays maybe, or the Isley Brothers. The woman has a lovely voice, but my inability to place the song prevents me from enjoying it. I know there's a lesson here, one I should heed, about dwelling in the now and the potter becoming his pot, et cetera. Instead I let the displeasure fester until I can't stand it anymore. I search a lyric on my phone and find the song: You Are Everything by the Stylistics. Covered later by Diana Ross and Marvin Gaye. They're covering the cover. The relief of not having to think about it anymore is close enough to pleasure. I pay our bill and we drive down the mountain.

Late afternoon and the day's talent fades as we listen to You Are Everything on repeat. I've got nothing incisive to say about it except that it's perfect. Better than Beowulf. Better than key lime pie. My son fiddles with the solar system bracelet in his lap. I remember I used ask him what he was thinking and he'd tell me without hesitation. He scrutinizes each colored orb. After some false starts and throat clearing, phrasing and rephrasing it in my head to make sound as neutral as possible, I ask him why he bought the bracelet for his ex-girlfriend.

Because I love her, he answers instantly.

The song finishes and begins again with Marvin Gaye and Diana Ross addressing each other with the blissful intimacy of a couple in bed.

That's beautiful, I say.

He waits for the punch line. I tell him I'm being serious. After a while he says, Can you play something else?

Near Santa Maria the palm-tree cell phone towers turn into evergreen cell phone towers. We enter a valley of bone-white turbines. Towering erratic clocks counting wind. At a gas station the clerk bangs a roll of dimes against the cash register and deftly guides the contents into the drawer. The dimes are shiny, newborn. I accidentally open the door to the beer cooler when I mean to open the door to the bottled water. Right church, wrong pew, she calls out. I make a note in my notes app. We head north.

The world's deadliest animal, he says, looking at his phone. Guess.
    Man, I say.
    Nope.
    Hippo.
    It's not a mammal.
    Some type of spider.
    Closer.
    Wild dog with a toothache.
    Not a mammal.
    Crow with an ice pick.
    Dude.

Cat with the nuclear codes.

Come on.

Just tell me.

Keep guessing.

Mosquito, he says a few miles later.

That was my next guess.

Is this about what you were expecting so far? he asks.

Sure. Maybe. I don't know. I'm just glad you came. Really.

He nods. Here's another, he says, by the time a child leaves for college ninety percent of the time they've spent with their parents is over.

He shows me the post on his phone: These Fourteen Facts Will Blow Your Mind! Even though I doubt its veracity, it still stings.

I emit a mumbly noise that means *that's interesting* and *that hurts* in my own secret tongue.

The color orange was named after the fruit, he says.

We'll just make the most of the time we have left, I say.

Sharks are older than trees, he says.

Conversation forensics. Parsing lines like an actor. Mulling volume and inflection. Watching fathers on TV and realizing much of what I know about fathers comes from TV. How they hold the morning paper. How they pause for the laugh track.

Realizing all my stories about him are retellings of truer stories. Hearing the ticker ticking. We're almost at 90 percent. Ruing how gleeful it makes him to be in possession of such a fact, deadly as a mosquito.

Read me another, I say.

Everything's fine, the other voice says. The quiet voice, the one that rarely speaks unless spoken to.

North to SLO, <u>beautiful</u> country, <u>beautiful</u> hotel called Earl Brown, he blabbed about JC, drunk, elevator door slammed on head.

We search for a hotel in San Luis Obispo called Earl Brown but there isn't one. So concludes the case of the missing comma. The most beautiful hotel in San Luis Obispo, according to the internet, is the Arroyo Grande. Rooms start at $398 a night so instead we stay at the Madonna Inn, a sprawling stone-and-stucco chalet off the 101. Hundreds of disconcertingly themed rooms. China Flower, Krazy Dazy, Sir Walter Raleigh. Ours is Antique Cars. Some rooms have gold-filigree ceilings and massive sleigh beds and fireplaces in walls of uncut stone. Ours has two double beds side by side and a few paintings of antique cars on the walls.

My son dumps his backpack on the bed and walks off to call his ex-girlfriend. I head to the pool, order a drink, and sit at the edge with my legs in the water. I send my wife the few pictures I've taken: scenery, our son biting into his sandwich, the singer's metal crutch, my legs in the water. Cars whir up and down the 101 and I try to imagine my father staying here, using the ice machine, pouring himself a plastic cup of scotch. Sitting on the end of his single bed, smoking menthols, and watching TV. Calling up Earl Brown. Talking about horses. My father making a mildly clever comment like *I don't like being drunk... but I do like getting drunk*. Earl Brown agrees with a grunt, then starts blabbing about JC—Jimmy Carter or Jesus—and my father hangs up and goes to pee and at the bowl realizes he's crossed the line between getting and being drunk, so he walks out into the night, into terrain so unlike Florida it may as well be Mars. Beautiful country, he thinks. He'd like to spend the rest of his life here. He's forty-five years old. The end is near—he could hear its approach if he listened closely. But he isn't listening. He's thinking about astronauts playing golf on the moon, wondering if it happened or if he dreamed it or saw in a movie. He thinks, *A day comes when a man is no longer welcome company for himself*. Then, *Jesus, I'm drunk*. He wanders off in the direction of an elevator and I let him go.

My son finds me at the edge of the pool with a second drink, working through the Sunday crossword on my phone. A timer marks how long it takes for the crossword to go from something I'm doing to something I've done. My son removes his shoes and socks and joins me. He wears an expression of discreet contentment, the look of someone being led into a surprise party he already knows about. I suspect he's been smoking weed, but I'm not going to say anything. I've been wrong before. I set my drink and phone down on the pool deck, take out my wallet and hand it to him, and then close my eyes and list forward slowly, slowly, until I'm face down in the water. I kick off from the wall and drift toward the middle of the pool into a patch of colder water and do the dead man's float for as long as I can. It's the sort of thing that, when he was little, would've made him hysterical with laughter. He's smiling when I resurface. How drunk are you? he says.

Not even two drinks drunk, I say, heaving myself up onto the edge. When I was a kid, I say, I never thought my parents were drunk. Though they usually were. I just thought people got happier at night. He gives me back my wallet and we sit there without talking as the chill night air seeps in.

I wake up before dawn feeling clearheaded, feeling like I've been granted a pardon after a long sentence. Looking at my son, who's lightly snoring in the other bed, a single parasitic earbud in his ear, I think, *Even the hardest days aren't so hard*. The birthday party when he ate bad sushi and we had to wait in the emergency room while he vomited into a shopping bag. The constant arguments during quarantine. The back and forth about him smoking weed. Today. Remember this, I always tell myself.

This clarity, this feeling of clemency that has everything to do with you and that you have nothing to do with. Remember it for when you need it next. But how do you remember a feeling?

Two missed calls from my mother, just past four a.m. One new voicemail.

Hi, honey. It's after seven... guess you're still asleep. They patched me up and now I'm home. Sitting here waiting to call the handyman to get rid of that cactus. I hate it. It doesn't even flower. I just remembered something you might be interested in. I love you so much, baby. I wish you'd call me back.

I listen to it in the café while waiting for coffee, then replay it. Her voice is soft, beseeching. Never before has she called me honey or baby, so either the call was meant for Elias Parker or overnight she has summoned a newfound tenderness toward me.

I call her back. Her phone rings once and goes to voicemail.

The waitress calls me sweetie. Today I guess I'll be the apple of everyone's eye. Her cheeks are covered with light freckles that intensify down her neck and into the collar of her uniform. She wears a ring on every finger, each with a different stone—brown stone, green stone, blue, bluer, red—and it stirs something, a wisp of feeling or memory, as she brings me coffee and orange juice. I wanted to sit in the café and collect some thoughts about the trip while my son sleeps in, but I'm distracted by the waitress's rings. Everything reminds me of something else.

The coffee tastes like urn. The orange juice tastes like can. Orange juice always makes me feel slightly ill because when I was a kid that's the only time my mother would buy it. I'd ask for juice and she'd pour me a glass of Sunny Delight. She preferred it over real orange juice even though she grew up within sniffing distance of the orange groves. She never had much truck with nature. She liked things that came in predictable shapes, things you could open: cans, bottles, boxes.

For Halloween one year I dressed as a box of Surf detergent. She thought it was so clever she sent a photo of me to the corporation that manufactures Surf. Three months later they mailed her a coupon for $1.50 off her next purchase. She was livid, she ranted about it for years... but what had she expected? Free Surf for life? She never could shed her faith in products she saw advertised on television. She knew Ivory was 99.44 percent pure and Calgon would take her away. These days I can hear her TV in the background when we talk on the phone. It's always tuned to the jewelry network, where the commercials are the show, and the shows are all about jewelry.

I sip orange juice in the café. I scribble. What do I have so far? Nothing I couldn't have come up with from home. Circus music. Solar system bracelet. My mother's disappointment with the wound clinic. I wonder what she'd expected. A koi pond?

A concierge? And does she really not remember who bought her the cactus?

I call the manager of her retirement home to ask if he can send someone to remove it. He says he already did. Someone stopped by her unit but she'd reconsidered. She likes it where it is. Your mother's a very spirited lady, he says, a slight barb in his voice. I'm sure you heard about the protest a few weeks back. I'm glad we reached a compromise.

The call concludes with awkwardly deployed pleasantries.

We sure are happy for your mother, he says.

Us too, I say.

The protest was over pesticides, she tells me when she calls back. She wanted the groundskeepers to stop spraying behind their building because egrets and ibises nest there. She radicalized some other residents and they all put homemade signs on their doors and wrote letters to the director of the retirement home. Finally the director gave in and they stopped spraying. She didn't tell me about it because she thought it would embarrass me. You know how you get, she says. These birds are incredible. I've seen them since childhood but Elias Parker had to point them out for me to notice them. I saw a roseate spoonbill the other day. It landed, opened its wings to sun itself, and flew off. None of the bird people here believe it. They're such snobs.

They say it's too far north for a spoonbill. I said, *Okay, then someone should tell* him *that.*

Elias Parker? I say.

No, she says, the bird people.

But who's *him*?

Back and forth we go until everything is tucked in and put to bed. Him is the spoonbill. She tells me her shin feels fine but since she started taking the pain meds she keeps hearing people on TV say her name. And, no, she can't explain why she changed her mind about the cactus. A voice told her to say no to whoever was knocking on her door so that's what she did. Did the people on TV tell you that? I ask. She doesn't laugh.

I bought her the cactus the last time I visited. It's a flowering ocotillo. The day before I flew out she said she had a surprise. She wouldn't tell me what it was. She didn't want to spoil it. Her coyness, the way she protected it, I suspected it involved my father, something she remembered or found.

I met her in her dining hall. I hadn't seen her in a year and was startled by how old she looked. She'd let her hair go fully gray and her eyes, usually clear bright blue, had dimmed. She had trouble standing up to hug me, so I leaned down and briefly put my arms around her and felt her body, somehow fragile and rigid at the same time.

Two men sat on either side of her, one in a hat with WHO RESCUED WHO stitched across it and the other wearing a pearl-button shirt. I'd been up since three a.m. and I started babbling about Blue Zones, regions in the world with high life expectancies. I watched a documentary on the airplane and I told them about a centenarian in Costa Rica who rides horses and chops firewood, while the man in the hat regarded me with open scorn between bites of chicken-fried steak. The key to longevity, I told them, in this part of Costa Rica, is all the work that needs to be done morning to night—if they died, who would do all the work? Also, it had something to do with corn.

Meet Elias Parker, my mother told me, gesturing to the man with the pearl-button shirt. He's a retired dentist. He's the one I told you about.

At this point I'd never heard the name Elias Parker in my life. I shook his hand and thought that was it, but he followed us back to her unit, came inside, and fixed himself a scotch at the sink. I whispered to her, Who is that? She repeated his full name and I said, No, what I mean is, who is he, like, to you? That's when she told me they're in love. I looked at him again, running his hand under the tap and flicking water into his scotch glass, and asked her, Is he aware of this?

We sat on her couches while they reminisced about high school. Or while she reminisced and Elias Parker interjected in his vaguely Hungarian accent: Oh yeah, we use to like zee dances. Remember passing notes in the hall? my mother said. Sure, Elias Parker said. Love notes. For me it's all so sweet like a dream.

* * *

I brought the cactus to the retirement home the next day. Instead of GUEST PARKING, the signs in front say FUTURE RESIDENT PARKING. A bit hopeful, a bit ominous. It calls to mind the chapel of bones in Évora. Arches filled with skulls and femurs, and an inscription: *Nos ossos que aqui estamos pelos vossos esperamos.* We, the bones that are here, await yours.

I gave her the cactus to remind her of our trip to Joshua Tree. When I fell? she said. Why would I want to be reminded of that? No, I said. That was in Mexico. The pharmacist gave you pills that made you hallucinate butterflies fluttering out of your bedspread. Remember?

I wish, she said.

She made Pillsbury biscuits. She liked to always have some on hand because they're Elias Parker's favorite. Waiting for them to bake she told me they were moving in together. That was the surprise. I'd forgotten about the surprise. They found a two-bedroom unit on the fourth floor with a view of the egrets and the ibises. He just needed to clear it with his niece. I reminded her how much she liked living alone. You're in the same building, I said. Isn't that enough?

We went back and forth until I lost track of what I was advocating for, or why. Who was I to get in the way of what they wanted? Finally she said, I want to do it soon. We're not getting any younger.

I'd heard this tired phrase dozens of times. But in her reedy voice in that tiny kitchen it resonated like the world's last discovered truth.

She reached out as if to give me something. When I opened my hand she clutched it and would not let go. A slap would've startled me less. Her hand was like a creature pulled from deep water: ice cold, alien, hard. It's the most sustained physical contact we've had since I was a baby. A minute and counting. I held my breath. Someone in the hallway sneezed. She let go.

I think he'd be okay with it, she said, don't you?

How sad, I thought, driving back to my hotel. Forty years on and she still cared about her dead husband's approval. Then I realized it wasn't his approval she was fishing for but mine. Reaching out for it, trying to seize it with her hand.

Later she called to tell me Elias Parker's niece nixed the idea. The niece complained to the manager of the retirement home that her uncle was coerced into a relationship against his will. For now, they'd have to take the elevator to rendezvous with their beloved.

We drive north past Morro Bay and Cambria. He woke up this morning grumpy and sluggish, so we didn't get on the road until almost noon. I bought him a muffin in the café and he sits with it in his lap. He keeps checking his phone. Finally, he flings it into the back seat and closes his eyes.

Everything okay? I say.
Couldn't be better, he says.
Anything you want to talk about?
He shakes his head.

We pull over in San Simeon for the elephant seals. About fifty of them lie roped off in the sand. He calls his mother, holds out his phone so she can see them. Two big ones face off, rearing their heads back. Bright pink mouths. My son points the camera at me, then at the barking seals, then back at me, then at the seals again, and laughs. He laughs with every muscle of his face and never for long, and when he stops it's like staring at a lightbulb while turning it off, laughter still glares around his face. He puts the phone to his ear and responds to her questions with whispered answers. The glare of laughter dissipates. He turns away, walks to the edge of the parking lot. I'm sure he's talking about me, complaining about the trip, wishing she hadn't made him come.

I watch a convertible's soft top snap unhinged like a snake's jaw. The waitress's rings, I remember what they remind me of. In third grade I had two teachers, Ms. Daniker and Ms. Danaher, who were as distinct from each other as a knife and a spoon. One sat behind her desk and stood up only to write on the chalkboard. The other walked around, sharpening our pencils with a paring knife because she hated the sound of the crank sharpener. One wept when Karen Carpenter died. She played her songs on the portable turntable we used for musical chairs. I was too anxious to appreciate the mournful beauty of her voice, too programmed to scurry for an open chair when the song stopped. The other wore a ring on every finger, even her thumbs.

Recently my wife suggested they were the same person. I admit the possibility had occurred to me. My wife thought they were a projection of my unconscious desires—one maternal, the other sexual—and since my young mind couldn't reckon them together, I split them into two women, which was not unnatural, not unhealthy... but I was only half listening. I was remembering how one woman would come to class smelling like cold cream. The other like nothing I could name.

You okay? I say when he returns.

Your zipper's down, he says.

Which means no. Possibly yes.

Hearst Castle: $2.50, 156 Greek vases. Neptune gold. Kin swim free. Expired transfer.

We pay sixty dollars for a guided tour of rooms fit for a demented king. Our guide wants us to know that William Randolph Hearst was a product of his time. Winston Churchill sat over there. Out the window you'll see the airstrip where Amelia Earhart landed. My son and I drift to the rear of the group. My mind wanders. I imagine my father walking through the castle counting vases. I wonder if he felt any pang or premonition as he toured room after room of a man's beloved opulent junk made into a museum. Foreseeing his own beloved junk, tools, golf clubs, letterman jacket, faux-leather recliner, packed up and shipped to his childhood home in Kentucky. Displayed in his old bedroom with a voice-over playing on a loop from hidden speakers: he loved horses, he could do unfathomable calculations in his head...

We walk around the Neptune Pool, which was used in the movie Spartacus. The inlay around the pool's edge is twenty-four-karat gold, the guide tells us. I ask him if Hearst's relatives swim free. No one swims here, he says. Not even Spartacus.

My wife texts me: *C feeling bad about L. Be easy with him.*

C is our son, L is his ex-girlfriend. Easy is what I need to be reminded to be. It's what I used to always write atop my notes for teaching: *BE EZ.*

That place is kind of awesome, my son says.

I pull over at a skate park. He wants to stay in the car. I don't argue. I'm being easy. I cruise around. My legs are wobbly and my trucks are too loose and the prefab ramps are covered in crumbling Masonite. It's okay. I am ageless. I've got the muscle memory of a thirty-six-year-old. Kids on scooters zip back and forth against the flow of the park. I drop in and almost collide with one of them. Off-balance, I try to boardslide the flat bar. I ollie up, lock in, and slip out and slam onto polished cement. The right kind of fall can be salubrious, but this isn't that kind of fall. I stay down. Sir, a kid on a scooter says, handing me my board. Do you need a hand, sir? It might be the strangest thing anyone's ever said to me.

When I stand up I see my son on the deck with his board. He watches me flail around trying the boardslide. I'm sore and ready to get back on the road but I'm not leaving yet. Another try and I slip out onto my back again. Some day I will fall like this, I say to myself, and I won't get up. I hear him drop in. At first I think he's coming to check on me but he takes two pushes and ollies over my legs. We aren't leaving until you land that, sir, he calls out. He smith grinds the flat bar, nose manuals the manual pad, kickflips up the euro gap. He expends great effort making it look effortless.

Finally I land it. I look up at him, watching something on his phone, uninterested. I feel sullen and dispirited as we pull back on the road. He still isn't talking.

Later he texts me the video he was filming from the deck: me looking like a hunchback, two pushes, paltry ollie, sad boardslide, then a needy glance at him on the deck. And again in slo-mo. Then just my corpulent head in super slo-mo. He's edited it to the Kinks song, the one he doesn't remember and used to love.

It probably felt better than it looks, he says, smiling.

He's right. Whatever pall that was hanging over him and me and the car lifts. For now. I ask him to play us a song, something I've never heard before.

That doesn't sound like you, he says, connecting his phone.

An irrational plan must be abandoned irrationally. On the dashboard is a button labeled AMB. Years ago, when we test drove the car, the salesman pointed to the button and said, That lets you adjust your ambiguity. My wife and I laughed but he was dead earnest. I decide that if our ambiguity is above sixty-five, I will quit following my father's route. If it's below, then we'll continue. I push it: 63, it reads. I push it every few miles. We remain at a steady sixty-three ambiguity all the way to Big Sur.

I thought reading the gray book along the way might add a spark, like eating seafood within view of the sea. I wasn't expecting a grand sentimental reckoning but maybe just a glimpse. There's been no glimpse, no seafood, no sea. My mother thinks I'd hardly think about him if he were alive. She says if I remembered him I'd have no trouble at all forgetting him.

San Simeon to Big Sur. More <u>beautiful</u> country. Piano at Deetjen's.

* * *

Aren't we stopping? he asks as we drive past Deetjen's.
    Let's skip it, I say.
    It's right there.
    I know.
    You're gonna regret it.
    Probably.

If I see an Arizona license plate in the next ten minutes I'll quit following his route. If the next song he plays has an NBA player's name in its lyrics. If I see five consecutive cars heading south with their headlights on, a black Mercedes, a pickup truck…

A Tacoma with crooked fog lights drives past, a sign from above. I push the AMB button: 66. So let it be written, so let it be done.

The rappers I used to listen to rapped about selling drugs, I tell him while a Yung Lean song plays from his phone. The ones you listen to rap about doing drugs.

He nods like he's listening. I'm not entirely sure what my point is, or if I'm just reminding him I'm still here.
    Can I ask you something? he says.
    Ask away.
    What's the worst thing you did when you were my age?
    Whoa.

Don't think about it, just answer.
The worst thing... like to someone?
Or yourself.
How about the best thing?
I can tell it's bad. I see it in your face.
Of course it's bad, it's the worst thing.

We slow down at the Point Sur Lighthouse, pull off at the falls. I leave the gray book in the car.

We walk along an outcropping and come upon a view that is literally breathtaking. I take pictures, look at them, and delete them because nothing captures it. We continue north. I tell him about writers who used to live here. Henry Miller, happy old lech. Richard Brautigan, who wanted to end a novel with the word *mayonnaise* but never did. He looks up the names on his phone as I'm talking about them. Richard Brautigan lived in Bolinas, he says.
    I hate when you do that.
    So are you gonna tell me or not?

What comes to mind is a memory from high school. It's not the worst thing but it's what comes to mind. While my mother was in class, I loaded up a bag with groceries she just bought, returned them to the store, and kept the money. She came home to make dinner and found things missing: cans of tuna, breadcrumbs, bacon bits. I played dumb when she asked what was going on. I can't remember seeing it, I said. Are you sure you didn't leave the bag in the cart? Returning the groceries was bad, but standing idly while she thought she was losing her mind, not enjoying it but not letting it bother me either, was worse. Not the worst thing, but what comes to mind.

Later a military recruiting officer started coming by, trying to convince me to go to Jacksonville to take the armed services vocational test. I'd agreed to take a practice test and he said I scored in the highest percentile. I was smarter than Norman Schwarzkopf. If I did well on the real test I could name my assignment: Navy SEAL, codebreaker. The officer played on my insecurities like an expert salesman. Even his compliments seemed incriminating: What an amusing young man you are, he told me. The second I saw you I knew you were the type who likes to amuse others. But I bet you know you're destined for a more challenging path than your peers.

He took me to lunch at Friendly's. As we waited to order he said, I had a vision last night. You, five years from now, flying support missions in a Black Hawk helicopter.

And then it occurred to me, as I tried to imagine myself even sitting in a helicopter, that he was full of shit. I would be the guy assigned to wash the helicopter. The guy assigned to wash towels for the guy assigned to wash the helicopter.

I stopped returning his calls and answering the door and he gave up. My mother later admitted she was the reason he started coming by. She thought I was rudderless. Maybe the military would give me a better sense of myself. This was as the first Gulf War was ramping up, a fact I reminded her of for years: Remember when you wanted me to go to the desert to fight Saddam? What do you want me to say? she'd reply.

I tell him this as we make our way north. He still likes stories from my reprobate days. Snack-machine larceny, plasma selling, waterbed hypothermia. He asks if I ever apologized to her and I tell him of course, but I can't remember if I even admitted what I'd done. It's hard to grow up without money, I say.

Must've been hard for her too, he says.

We pass a van with a HOW'S MY DRIVING? bumper sticker. In Florida, I say, I used to see cars with the same bumper sticker and the number 1-800-EAT-SHIT. That passed for fiendish wit in Florida, I tell him.

He says he's imagining her going back to the store and buying the same groceries again, only for me to sell them back again. Like Sisyphus and his boulder, he's thinking. What a little shit, he's thinking. Actually I have no idea what he's thinking.

I only did it once, I say.

* * *

I did it several times, come to think of it. Who knows what I spent the money on. I remember coming home from Pizza Hut with friends and sneering at some grievous taco casserole she'd kept warm for me. I don't think I'd be so callous that I'd spend the grocery money on Pizza Hut when she had food ready at home, but I wouldn't bet against it.

If it isn't the worst thing, why did it come to mind? And why include the military recruiter, which happened over a year later? Do you think it cancels out what you did? That it somehow pardons you?

I forgot to mention that when I visited her in Florida we drove to our old town house because she wanted to take a picture of me out front. She still remembered our years there fondly. Stopped at a red light, she turned down the radio, waited, and turned it up again. I just wanted to see if the radio is what was bothering me, she said. And? And it isn't, she said. Also I forgot about the bowl of condoms in the lobby of her retirement home. The manager saw me looking at them. STDs, he said. And the sestina about my father, moved from the bathroom of her condo to the bathroom of her retirement home. And the composition book she set out on her coffee table when she first moved there.

On the cover it said *Interesting Facts About Sex After Age 70*. Inside the book were blank pages. And the smell of urine in the dining room. I always scold students when they write stories set in nursing homes that smell like urine. I forgot to mention the insides of her cabinets covered in Post-it notes: *Remember you already told CP you love him. Don't call him back!!!* And: *I am one lucky gal!! My son never hangs up the phone without saying love you, mom.* The handwriting is hers but the brittle optimism, the multiple exclamation points, these are new. The flush of tenderness I felt when I read it.

The Post-it note with my telephone number on it—after the number is my name. After my name is what I am: *Son.*

She had trouble picking out our town house. She knew we lived on the end but couldn't remember which end.

You think the Howells still live back there? she said. I don't remember the Howells, I said. Really? she said. You used to sit on the back porch listening to them. They made the fiercest racket the day he died.

In Monterey my father ate broiled monkfish at Mo's. My son and I go to the aquarium on the Bay and gaze at fish swimming in strangely lit tanks. We wander from exhibit to exhibit, testing our stamina for reverence. We pet manta rays in a kiddie pool. We watch penguins violently mating and immortal jellies that look like globs of bloody mucus. Greedy otters. Schooling sardines. The octopus stops us. We don't read about its habits from the placard, we just want to see it bloom and writhe. Its strangeness silences us, for a while. An octopus in Chile, a woman says, predicted the last three presidents. Chilean? I ask. American, she says. Amazing, I say, that it even knows who the candidates are. My son rolls his eyes. The octopus reemerges and a boy slaps the tank glass and the octopus's skin seethes orange and we are silenced again, for a while.

At the gift shop I tell my son to pick something out. Whatever he wants. He looks around. I hold up an aquarium-themed Monopoly game. He shakes his head. A wind-up anglerfish. Nope. A blue whale puppet. He isn't seven. I stand at the puppet bin with a whale on each hand. I make them whisper nonsense to each other. Secrets of the deep, I say. He stares at me blankly.

He hands me a bottle opener key chain and I buy it for him. He drops it into some inner pocket of his backpack as we're pulling onto the highway.

Stuck in traffic outside San Jose, listening to separate songs. Every few minutes his phone screen comes alive and his thumbs move across it, conjuring messages with impossible speed. I'm tempted to ask him about his worst thing, but I don't want to make him lie to me. I probably don't want the truth either. He removes one of his earbuds, cleans it on his pant leg, and puts it back in. You want to see the real me? he asks. Yes, I say. He doesn't hear me, he's just singing along. You're by my side but are you really with me? he sings. Yes, I say.

My mother calls. Her voice is hoarse. Elias Parker is moving to a retirement home in Orlando, she says. His niece is making him. She thinks I'm after his money. Do you believe that? I've got plenty of money.

You've got a little money, I say.

My son smacks my leg. You're on speaker, I say.

Helpless, she says. I'm helpless. You just put me here and forgot about me.

I didn't put you there, Mom. You sold your condo because you wanted to downsize.

That's how you remember it.

Her responses seem rehearsed for a more demanding audition. I turn to my son, who's staring at me like *do something*.

What does Elias Parker say about this? I ask.

He's heartbroken. But it's his niece. Did I tell you what she does for a living?

You did.

She's a big deal in Kissimmee.

We'll take care of it, my son says.

Who is that?

It's me. Your grandson. We'll make some calls. Don't worry about it.

Oh, I'm not worried, she says, suddenly placated. I'll be fine. How are you?

They talk about the weather, his last year of high school, his girlfriend. He answers her questions. He doesn't tell her they're not together anymore. Before hanging up she says, Will you put your father back on?

I'm right here, Mom.

Could you please *please* not tell him about this? she says.

You're on speaker, I repeat, and she whispers, Tell him I'm sad because one of my oldest friends died.

We'll make some calls? I say.

You weren't doing anything, he says.

I remember the last time she stayed with us in California. We drove her to the desert because she'd always had a soft spot for unusual flora and had never seen a Joshua tree. I parked at the easiest trailhead I could find but it was too steep—she worried about her ankles buckling. Go on without me, she said. Take my arm, our son said. He guided her, pointing out Joshua trees and tortoise burrows and the rock where Gram Parsons's friends tried to cremate his body after stealing it from LAX. I was reminded of how embarrassed of her I was at his age: driving to school with her, pulling up next to some kid in my class, and ducking down as if looking for something on the floorboard. Pretending not to hear her when she called for me in a busy store. It took years for this shame to subside. On the way home she reached in her purse and handed my son a twenty-dollar bill and pointed to her cheek and he kissed it.

San Francisco, the end of the line. We check in to our rental in Presidio Heights. I take off my shoes and lie down on the couch. We'll get dinner in a minute, I tell him. I fall asleep instantly. When I wake up he's eating a burrito at the kitchen table. I ask where it's from and he holds up a Chipotle bag. He knows what's coming, rant #48h (eating a homogenized version of a food in the city that is famous for it), a variation on #48 (fast food in general). I stay quiet. He doesn't need to hear it again.

    I saved you some chips, he says.

The next morning we wander the city. Without a plan, without the gray book to follow, one place seems as good as any. Bison in the park, sea lions at the wharf, giant spools of underground cable-car cable at the depot. We bicker about where we want to eat and end up at a sandwich place where neither of us wants to eat. We play pinball at the Musée Mécanique and walk around Embarcadero Plaza, skateboarding mecca in the nineties.

I tell him again about the summer some friends and I drove here from Florida in my old Civic: holes in the floorboards, CHECK ENGINE light blinking. We'd watched hours of skate videos filmed at the plaza and we knew every inch of it. Three-stair, seven-stair, C-block. A guy in a Newport jacket introduced himself as the mayor of EMB and said we needed to pay him twenty dollars each or be on our way. My friend Robby started skating and when his board shot out, the mayor flung it into the fountain. We paid him and skated for a few hours, sprained an ankle, cracked a fish-eye lens, and left to find a motel in the Tenderloin. My friends' parents bought them plane tickets home and I drove back alone. A four-day drive, the longest four days of my life.

I film him skating the plaza over bricks pockmarked into cobblestone by years of truck axles. You drove here for this? he says.

It was a pilgrimage, I say. It's all I had.

I wouldn't drive two miles for this.

Well, you wouldn't have to. If you wanted to come here, I'd drive you.

Sure. But this place is pretty dead.

I don't mean *here* here. A place like here.

We sit on the three-stair and watch a man film his friend scaling the giant metal sculpture spewing water into the fountain.

He says, Were drugs more powerful back then?

* * *

We didn't take drugs, I tell him. We were high on self-loathing. I'd told my mother I was visiting colleges. After five days of not hearing from me, she called the police, hospitals, friends' parents. Finally Robby's mom told her where we were. What I'd done was unforgivable, she said when I got home, but she forgave me.

Back when I was out late in high school she always said she couldn't sleep until I came home. I never believed her. Now when my son stays out late I think: *Of course she couldn't*. I didn't believe her when she told me she worried about me all the time. There was no sentiment, not even a simple *I love you*, that was beyond suspicion. I couldn't wait to leave home but soon after I got to college, I was so homesick I caught a ride home for the weekend. It was my bedroom I was homesick for, I told myself. Sure. The beanbag chair, Ed's old tape deck, giant whale mural forever smiling down.

I wish I could remember the stories I told Robby to keep us awake on our drive to California. Abjectly sentimental stories about my father, intended to break his heart. He did start sobbing. I felt powerful. A friend in the back seat woke up and asked why Robby was crying. He wiped his eyes. Because, he said, quickly recovering, this poor fucker's dumping out his life story. I'm crying at him, not with him.

* * *

We go to Sausalito. On the ferry I argue with a Frenchman who won't take his bags off the seat next to him. My son gets mad at me for getting mad at the Frenchman. He mimics my bitchy incoherent retort, *Oh, yes, look how comfortable they are.* I try to find the captain—sometimes a ship captain brings everything into focus… but there is no captain, just a guy in a T-shirt turning knobs. At the stern I stare into the wake, thinking haphazard thoughts about fathers and sons—the wake, eddying into the surrounding chop, dissolution, transmigration, life. A flock of birds trails behind the ferry, weaving, gliding, resisting analogy. My mother calls. I don't pick up. A few minutes later she calls my son and he looks at his phone and looks at me. I shrug. He answers.

I hear her on the other end. She says she's been sad since one of her oldest friends died. He tells her we're on a ferry near the Golden Gate Bridge and she says how happy it makes her that he gets to see the world. One of her biggest regrets was never having money to take me anywhere, not even the Grand Canyon. Did he know that his father used to be obsessed with the Grand Canyon? Canyons, gorges, trenches, I was a fan of rifts in the earth. I don't remember, but I know parents preserve what their children forget. He stays on the phone until we dock in Sausalito. He mostly listens.

* * *

What are we going to do? he says.

We eat lunch, we eat ice cream, we take the ferry back. I buy my wife a scarf. He buys his ex-girlfriend a scarf. He browses shoes at a skate shop on Haight. The kid at the counter has a tattoo of a Bukowski quote about intelligent people and stupid people. I ask if he's read Fante and, taken aback, he says, Why are you asking? I'm writing a monograph, I want to say, on the reading habits of skate-shop employees, but my son's within earshot, so I point to the tattoo. We go to City Lights. He snaps a picture of himself pretending to read Infinite Jest and sends it to his mother. It saddens me irrationally. We return to the apartment, we argue about what to watch, we watch The Big Sleep, we sleep. I dream punishment and he dreams escape. We go to a skate park beneath an overpass. A kid tries to nosegrind the channel and falls on his wrist. He holds it up for his friends, thumb bent nauseatingly out of joint. Think it's broken? he says giddily. He smokes half a joint and skates off. Hard not to admire his showmanship. We keep moving. We walk around Lands End, the Mission, Buena Vista Park. We meet people. I write down a snatch of graffiti: *he who doesn't know truth is the looser.* I keep telling myself there's something else we should be doing.

* * *

He leaves for college in eighty-seven days. He can cook salmon and eggs and rice and beans. He can parallel park. He knows how to behave in an earthquake. He has fallen in love. I haven't taught him how to change a tire or sharpen a knife. (I don't know how to sharpen a knife.) I've told him to run in a zigzag when chased by an alligator and swim parallel to the shore when caught in a riptide. I've told him to write dispatches to himself in ten years to keep in touch with earlier versions: the boy who feared snakes, the one who made mazes and bought souvenirs for a girl he loved. He knows how to read a map. He leads us to a market in Chinatown to buy loose mango tea for his ex-girlfriend. In the back of the store, hanging above a dim hallway, is a sign that says NEVER ENDING QUAILS. Tentatively he walks down the hall, tentatively I follow.

I want to walk back to the apartment—he wants to catch a cab. Can't see the city in a cab, I say. We've walked sixteen thousand steps today, he says. His phone will back him up. But he lets me get my way. We walk through Russian Hill, up Lombard, into Cow Hollow and the Presidio. He asks why we're on this death march and I say it's good to do things you don't want to do and he says why's that and I say contrast.

Great, he says when we come upon a fountain topped by a statue of Yoda. We've reached fucking Dagobah. Do you even know where we are? We're seeing the city, I say, we're working up an appetite, I say, we're racing the sun, but I have no idea.

* * *

Deeper into the Presidio, beneath a split overpass we come upon a hundred ramshackle headstones surrounded by a picket fence. It looks like a Halloween display. We walk along a winding path, past a sign saying PRESIDIO OF SAN FRANCISCO PET CEMETERY. Did you know this was here? he asks. I say I'm as surprised as he is. We read the inscriptions. *The Champ. Caramel. The Love You Gave Won't Be Forgot.* My son kneels down to take pictures. Best boy, he reads.

I step lightly along the bumpy ground. The headstones all look handmade and are at least thirty years old. Some have been repainted and probably re-repainted. I search for the longest surviving animal. Fifteen-year-old dog, seventeen-year-old cat, twenty-two-year-old unspecified. At the back of the lot, planted cockeyed, is a faded white headstone that reads: *Candy. '68–'78. Good egg.*

I don't need the gray book to remember.

Atop the plot are flourishing shrubs shaggy with red and yellow blossoms. Two different shrubs from the look of it, growing into each other.

Helped dig, he wrote. *Candy. Good egg.*

You can't still be upset, can you? a woman says. For a second I think she's speaking to a dead pet, then I notice the earbuds.

Cold wind blows in an odor of woodsmoke. I zip my coat and kneel on the footpath next to the shrubs and in a flash

I see it. My father at the cemetery gate. His hair is tousled, his zipper's halfway down, and his shoes are all wrong. Who knows what he's doing here, but clearly he hasn't found what he was looking for on this trip. Across the field a soldier is digging with a small bundle by his feet. My father clears his throat and calls out, Need some help?

That's it. That's what I see. Not the digging or the burying, just the offer. Him walking over and reaching out for the shovel, the split second of uncertainty before the soldier hands it to him and he makes himself useful.

I dig my fingers into the dirt, scoop up a handful, and release it. A chaos of shoeprints crisscrosses in the dirt path, but not his shoeprints surely, no, certainly not his.

I start to call my son over. He's talking to an elderly man with a pair of springer spaniels. He leans down and they lick his face. No need to summon him. Let it flash, scoop up another handful, let it go.

They have relatives here, my son says, nodding to the dogs snuffling between the headstones. The man said they always go to the same place and sit there and won't budge. He and I wait for them to sniff their way to it.

Back at the apartment I say, Fourteen hours left. What do you want to do? Eat, he says. Then eat we shall, I say. He eyes me warily. You pick, I say. Burritos in the Mission or sushi or Vietnamese. We can take a cab, a trolley, or a rickshaw, whatever you desire. He finds an expensive seafood restaurant in Pacific Heights with a five-course menu. I suspect he chooses it just to mess with me but I offer no resistance. Five courses? I say. Hope it'll be enough. We catch a cab. As we wait for our table I see my mother has called. I listen to her message as I stare at a giant painting of a dilapidated boat tied to a dock, water lapping at its sides, beneath a sky full of harmless clouds.

It's me, she says in the message. I ate dinner in my unit tonight. There's supposed to be a Hitchcock marathon—I'm looking for it right now but I can't find it. It rained all afternoon. Then the clouds passed and the sun came out and it kept raining. I opened the sliding glass door and pulled up a chair and sat thinking I'm lucky. Lucky in some ways. Ms. Kim next door has three sons and none speak to her. She's leaving all her... aha! I found it... no, this is in Spanish. I just have to keep reminding myself how lucky I am.

Every time I look at the painting on the wall I notice some new element, a poorly mixed color or error of symmetry. And why's the water so choppy and the sky so clear?

    I'm lucky, she said. Lucky in some ways.
    What are we going to do? I say.

* * *

Amber kaluga caviar
Sashimi
Crab
Black cod
Smoked cream gelato

Between the first and second course my son takes out his phone. I think he's going to text his ex-girlfriend but instead he makes a call. His expression is tentative, childlike. It's me, Grandmére, he says in a low voice. He tells her where we are and describes the first course. I hear her exclaim *caviar!* on the other end. With crispy potato, he says, reading the menu, and crème fraîche. Very salty, he says. Four out of ten. He listens. I can't tell what she's saying but he smiles and doesn't look up. I'll call you back after the next course. Don't go to sleep, okay? Promise?

She promises. We wait for the next course. Two days from now we will return home and I'll call Elias Parker's niece to convince her to let her uncle stay at the retirement home. I'm prepared for a combative conversation but the niece is congenial and straightforward. She says she's a gastroenterologist—knitting organs is just a hobby. She tells me her uncle just got some bad news: he has cancer for the ninth time. It might be a world record, she says. She wants him closer so she can take care of him. He's afraid to tell my mother—he doesn't want to upset her. I mumble my condolences. Before I hang up I ask where he's from.

Greece originally, she says, but he grew up in Daytona. I think he and your mom went to high school together.

Salmon, my son tells her. Raw. I ate most of it. It's okay. He pauses to listen to her questions. I know what she wants to hear. Nothing pleases her like an expensive disaster. Yeah, it's a little gross. He tries to describe what it tastes like. The greasiness of the salmon, the dirt tang of the mushrooms and yuzu. I can see her in her kitchen, sipping a glass of Gallo wine with ice, transfixed.

He leaves for college. Across the country, twenty-five hundred miles from the edge of the California desert. I write him a long earnest letter and am in tears by the time I finish. It's the first time something I've written has made me cry. Nothing oblique or clever. I tell him he's the best thing that ever happened to me. I fight the urge to replace it with a more artful line. I give him the letter after he's settled into his dorm, before we leave to catch our flight. I don't know if he reads it. Days later he sends me a text with one red heart and one black heart. When I call him and it goes to voicemail, I listen to his outgoing message, the same one I overheard him recording and rerecording in his bedroom when he got his phone: Christmas day, age fourteen, an early whiff of the essential masquerade of the adult world. I think about how I always chastise students when they write about characters listening to voicemails of their children and dead spouses. I hang up before the beep.

The crab is served with prawn and summer squash and it's delicious. We laugh about how when my mother goes to restaurants she always says she's not hungry and then orders the most abject thing on the menu: blackened meatloaf, corn-dog lollipops, clam bites. She'll nibble at it then put her napkin over the plate like a sheet at a crime scene. Terrible, she'll say, invigorated. He calls her. A man at a nearby table makes a throaty sexual sound after finishing his first course. His face is maximally tan. Pretty good, my son is saying. He listens and looks at me and says she wants to know what I think about the crab. Tell her it tastes like they got it from a can, I say. He does. She loves that. I knew she would. Two more to go, he says, pray for us, and hangs up.

I quit fabricating memories. I remember what I remember. One of the last mornings my father and I spent together, before he lost consciousness and the ambulance came and took him to the hospital for good: drinking coffee and writing notes. His ashen face. Paintbrush of reddish hair. He hands me a slip. *Know what names that bird?* it says. He points to the window in the direction of the gumbo-limbo tree in our side yard. I look. There is no bird. He's writing another note when I turn back to him. He hands it to me. *Never mind.*

Neither of us touches our dessert. We sit becalmed while the gelato melts. He tries a tentative spoonful and as I watch him it occurs to me that my experience of this meal is secondary to his, a feeling some parents must have all the time, and one I've had before but never this acutely. It will pass. In the morning we pack our things and load the car. We aim ourselves south. As we're leaving San Francisco he reads the last entry in the gray book out loud.

Landing gear, sunset, dropped cigarette.

Two years later I help my mother move into the assisted-living wing of her retirement home. In the lobby of her building I see the flowering ocotillo flourishing in a new planter, studded with crimson blooms. My mother's new room has a TV mounted to the wall. Nothing in the room is hers except for the bed and the nightstand with three photographs on it: one of me and my wife, one of her grandson, and one of her with my father at the beach looking tan and handsome and giddy. The day she pinpointed as the happiest of her life, the day they got engaged. She asks me to buy her a bottle of scotch—her doctor has forbidden her to drink alcohol—and I do. I drink from a paper cup and she drinks from her last mug. Elias Parker dies in Orlando. No one mentions it to her. Can you hear the ocean? she asks, and even though the ocean is five miles east I tell her I can, faintly. We watch the jewelry network—for every new item we say yes or no depending on whether we would or wouldn't wear it. We part. She has trouble summoning my name, but she knows me and there is love in her eyes.

Remember our town house? Remember the back patio with the terrazzo floor? Snakes in their burrows below and owls in the pine trees. The owls made a fierce racket the morning he died. You sat on the patio with a comic book, listening. There's trouble afoot in the owl kingdom, you kept saying to yourself. You came to my room and saw me ironing the only black dress that still fit me, and I couldn't figure out how to tell you, so I decided that when you asked why I was ironing, that's when I'd do it, I'd say it as directly as I could and comfort you afterward. But you never asked. You wanted to talk about owls.

ABOUT THE AUTHOR

KEVIN MOFFETT is the author of two short story collections, as well as *The Silent History*, a narrative app for mobile devices. His work has been awarded the National Magazine Award, the Nelson Algren Award, and a literature fellowship from the National Endowment for the Arts. He teaches in the creative writing program at the University of Virginia and lives in Charlottesville.